The Magic Wallet:

Beginnings

By Matthew Roberts

You were trying to busy yourself by wandering the aisles of the dingy, somewhat depressing thrift shop. Everything in it was old, battered or just plain weird. Any one of those reasons being why these objects had found themselves into their new depressing home, and surely they'd stay in this place forever if not for eccentrics like your mother.

Wandering around several aisle over, picking through everything with a menacing glint in her eye, like a hawk, searching for it's prey, was your mother, the only reason you were here. You wouldn't call her crazy or even tasteless, in fact she always dressed like a woman half her age, which to her credit, she could pull off. But like all mothers, if it was cheap she wanted it. Unfortunately nothing in this shop was cheap enough. She hadn't found anything so far, not that that seemed to dampen her spirits and her gentle smile.

For your part you were just trying to be a good son and give her a lift, and to be 'the muscle' if she found anything good. Honestly, she probably just wanted to spend time with you, which was sweet, but this wasn't the kind of place you wanted to spend your entire Saturday.

And what the hell was that? You power walked over to

a shelf and smiled at your find.

A lamp shaped like a monkey and the light bulb went up its butt. Hard to guess why someone would get rid of that. It would look great on someone else's end table. Maybe you could buy it for one of your sisters?

"Forty-five" You scowled at the price tag. You didn't hate your money that much.

You weren't going to throw around that much cash for a one time gag that would very likely end up in the garbage an hour or two later. With a derisive sigh you put the lamp back and looked over the low shelves towards your mother. She still had half the store left and she was making sure she didn't miss anything. All you could do was waste time looking around for more weird shit.

You strolled through the aisles, giving everything a quick glance over, but you weren't finding anything that could hold your attention for more than thirty seconds, so you were making quick work of the store, quickly approaching your mother even after sweeping through every aisle behind her. That's when at the opposite end of the aisle she was perusing, something caught your eye.

Shoved to the back of the shelf, behind some chipped decorative glasses was a small leather square. You stuck your arm deep into the shelf and pulled it back. It was a simple looking wallet. Tan, with dark brown thread embroidering the edge. That was almost it except for a tiny, minimalistic devil sewn into a corner, its tail was designed to look like it was also the embroidery around the edge of the wallet. It looked brand new. And it was a measly five bucks.

Your own wallet was starting to get pretty ratty, sure it did the job so you hadn't seriously thought about replacing it, but you were considering it now. As you deliberated, you opened it up and your eyes lit up. Unceremoniously crumpled up and shoved roughly into the wallet was a disheveled five dollar bill.

"Find anything sweetie?" Your mother, at some point noticed you paying close attention to something and came towards you, practically beaming at the idea you might've found something on your little outing together.

You hesitated a moment, deep down you knew it was wrong, this was a charity shop on top of everything... and yet...

"Free wallet." You smiled back, pocketing the cash.

You couldn't be bothered to care. Weird....

Your mother's smile faltered a little at that, but she didn't say anything.

"You still want to look around, or you want to head out." You continued.

Your mother scanned the store for a moment before deciding,

"I'm not sure if I'm going to find anything good today."

"How about lunch then? My treat." You wiggled the wallet at her playfully.

Her smile came back brighter than before, so you went up front to pay for your purchase.

The cashier, half asleep on a stool at the counter was likely in the store for the first of the three possible reasons, but as she heard you approach perked up as best she could and gave you a warm grandmotherly smile.

"Just the wallet dearie?"

"Yes, thank you." You smiled back and reached into

your pocket for the gritty five dollar bill you had scavenged.

"I'll be outside." Your mother said behind you, trailing an arm across your shoulder as she headed to the door.

You nodded to her and handed over the beaten up bill over to the cashier.

The moment she touched the bill you were suddenly overwhelmed by the thought of just jumping the counter and bending her --

Gross! She was like a million years old, at least! One good thrust and you'd turn her to dust!

"You have a good day dearie!" The woman behind the counter smiled to you, closing her cash drawer and snapping you out of your thoughts.

You smiled back and headed straight for the door. The fuck was that? You've had weird intrusive thoughts before, you were pretty sure everyone had, but that one came out of fucking nowhere. You were still trying to scrub your mind when your mother fell in step beside you,

"So, where're we heading?"

"Uh…" You honestly hadn't thought that far, but this was downtown, you couldn't walk a hundred feet without finding an eatery of some sort, "How 'bout there?" You pointed towards the end of the street at what looked like an old fashioned diner.

Your mother didn't have any complaints, in fact she seemed quite overjoyed, probably that you weren't treating her to fast food. Money was tight for a college student, especially one that just got laid off due to cutbacks, so you probably would've gone for a cheap burger normally, but you had been so preoccupied with your thoughts you just pointed to the first place you spotted.

Once inside the building your suspicions were correct, it was an old fashioned diner. The lights were dimmed, the windows had their shades drawn, giving it a 'cozy feel.' There was a long bar in the center of the building, lined with stools and with a cash register set up on the end nearest to the door. And lining the walls was a multitude of old junk they probably got from the thrift shop you just left.

The place was pretty busy, mostly filled with old people

and a handful or two of businessmen, but the diner was clearly doing well for itself. Your mother ended up leading the way to a small booth, designed for four most likely, but it was the smallest table available. As you holed up in the corner against the window you looked around and noticed some old fashioned posters lining one of the walls. To your amusement one of them was without a doubt taken from the Fallout series.

"How are you folks doing today!" A chipper voice appeared beside you, the sheer volume of it startled you.

Standing at the side of your table, menus in hand was a bubbly looking teen. She had long wavy brown hair, it looked permed, like out of a nineteen-fifty's housekeeping magazine. She was wearing a baby blue smock with white polka dots, and it sported puffy sleeves that barely covered her slender biceps, and around her waist was a small apron with a pocket on the front. The dress didn't even make it to her knees, but her slender legs were covered by opaque white stockings, with a pair of baby blue high heels on her feet.

You somehow doubted a food service restaurant like this would make footwear as unstable as high heels a part of the uniform.

The only thing on her that didn't look like it was pulled straight out of the fifties was her very modern braces on her otherwise perfect pearly white teeth, which you got a real good look at since she wouldn't stop smiling broadly. The other out of place article was her glasses. They were comically large, thick rimmed, hipster-esque things. If you saw her glasses on a shelf you'd have scoffed at the idea anyone would willingly wear them, but seeing them on this girl they suited her, gave her the whole sexy nerd look.

"My, now that's fast service." Your mother smiled back at the beaming girl.

True, you had barely sat down and a waitress had appeared out of nowhere. You hadn't seen any staff when you looked over the place a moment earlier.

"Of course!" The girl shouted again, bouncing on the balls of her feet, part way out of her heels, "We pride ourselves on good customer service here!"

You were more prepared for it this time, but you were still a little put off by how loud she was. Sure there were quite a few people in the shop, but they were all having their conversations at a sensible volume. Based on the lack of reaction however, you assumed this girl was always like this.

"D'you need menus?" She boomed, and after you gave a quick nod, she brandished the laminated books at you and your mother, "Can I get you anything to drink?"

Your mother got a water, but you picked coffee. After confirming that was everything for now, the girl practically skipped off, her wavy locks bouncing with every step.

You couldn't help smirking at the overly chipper girl, and turning to you mother, about to say something about it, but she whispered at you first,

"That was Morgan Shenbaum." Your mother was leaned in conspiratorially.

"Okay…." You frowned a little. Was that name supposed to mean something to you?

"She's in a bunch of Dana's classes."

You nodded politely. Dana was your younger sister, eighteen and on her last year of high school. You were a little surprised that this girl was the same age as your sister, between her old fashioned clothes and hairstyle, and her geeky 'accessories' you were having a little trouble pinning down an age. Beyond that however you weren't sure how you were supposed to react to that information. Luckily you didn't really have too.

Whirling out of the kitchen and up to your table in what was surely record time, was Morgan, your waitress, setting down your drinks, still smiling.

"You folks decided on anything yet?"

And still loud.

You were caught off guard yet again, you wanted to say it was still from your experience in the thrift shop, but you had nearly shook that thought free by this point, you were just surprised by how into this job the girl was, you hadn't even opened your menu yet.

Your mother ended up saying something to that effect, sending the girl on her way with a chipper 'Take your time!' so you both could give the menu a once over.

The moment you both had decided before you even closed up your menus the girl was back, like a ninja. You were starting to consider she was a mind reader, or at least eavesdropping.

You sent her back to the kitchen awkward conversation with your mother resumed.

"Can I see that wallet you bought?"

You unhesitatingly handed it over. After turning it over in her hands for a bit she handed it back,

"Cute. You gonna switch over to it now?"

You honestly hadn't planned on it, but as you were about to say so you realized there was literally no reason you couldn't, not even your super waitress could make food cook faster, you had time to kill.

You started to move over your cash, debit card, etc, in the process you noticed a leather sleeve inside, with a clear plastic window, you considered placing your driver's license in it, but on a whim chose instead your student I.D. The moment you slid the I.D. into the sleeve, you were kind of glad you didn't put in something that you'd ever need to take out on any kind of regular basis the plastic card fit so snugly you'd probably destroy the sleeve in the process.

Then your stomach soured.

You felt queasy, and a little dizzy, and your face was

getting really hot something you evidently weren't doing a good job of hiding,

"Something the matter?" You mother asked, her gentle smile gone.

"No, just, super hungry I guess?" You weren't sure, it came out of nowhere and reasonably, you've felt hungry before, this was different, but you didn't want to worry her.

It helped though that even as you spoke you were starting to feel quite a bit better.

"Are you sure?"

"Yeah, mom, I'm fine." You were really starting to get back to normal again.

But what the hell was that all about?

"You folks doing okay?" Morgan had returned, her smile had shrunk considerably though.

"Yeah, fine." You quickly replied, before your mother could say anything.

"You look a little pale." Came the calm reply at a

surprisingly normal decibel.

You averted your gaze, not keen on being pitied but yet another person for something that really wasn't a problem anymore.

Looking down you couldn't help paying extra attention to how short this girl's dress was. It made it halfway to her knees, and this slender girl was prancing around like this all day, not a care in the world at who saw…. Just then her dress started to ride up a little bit.

Just a little more and….

"I think I know what you need!"

You were startled to say the least. You were of course shocked at your own uncharacteristically obvious leering, no matter how cute she was you weren't normally that blatant, but the bubbly girl had also gone back to shouting, and most of all, the reason her skirt started to ride up was because she was now kneeling on the bench beside you, her face mere inches from your own.

"W-what?" You were so engrossed with her dress and the small expanse of her slender, creamy thighs exposed between the tops of her stockings and the hem of her dress, that you didn't realize she'd been getting so much closer.

A quick glance to your mother for a bit of help ended up being quite fruitless, she was busy giving you a disapproving glare.

"Your food's gonna be another few minutes, so how about I help occupy your time?" Morgan's broad, bubbly smile was replaced with a tight lip smirk, though her loud, chipper voice was still the same.

You were at a loss, until you felt a soft hand running up your thigh, stopping once it reached your fly. You quickly swatted the girl's hand away and hissed at her,

"What are you doing?" You gave your mother a sharp look but her frown hadn't gotten any worse.

"I'm sorry, I just thought a blowjob might help you relax." The girl looked absolutely devastated.

The look did not suit her. She was made to smile, not frown, and certainly not over not getting to suck dick, she looked far too innocent for that.

"M-mom?" Your main concern though was the fact that your mother was two feet away when one of your sister's classmates just tried to pull your sausage out in the middle of a crowded restaurant.

"You promised to pay, so I guess you can do what you want." She shrugged, while taking a dainty sip of her water

Huh? Your brain just kind of shorted out. Did you hear that right? You were expecting disgust, maybe even shock or embarrassment. Hell, absurd as it would've been, a high five would've been more in line with your expectations than that. In your family you liked to tease each other, your mother being no exception for either side of the equation, but she was the biggest prude in your entire family, this should've been fazing her just as much as you, if not more.

"I-I didn't mean to upset you, is there anyway I can make this up to you?" Morgan rushed through her sentence, hands over her mouth, tears welling up in her eyes, as she sat back onto her heels.

"You, uh, tried to pants me in front of all these people…." You stupidly worked your mouth.

You were getting whiplash from her sudden mood swing, she was so flirty a second ago and now she was acting like she accidentally murdered your entire family.

"I… I thought you could use… how else would I suck you off?" Morgan stammered, looking almost as confused as you felt.

"Haha, yeah, I guess that makes sense." You didn't even know what you were saying anymore.

Morgan looked a little less stressed out however when you chuckled a little.

"I'm really sorry though." She mumbled again.

"Oh stop tormenting the poor girl." Your mother gave you a tight lipped smile.

Huh? That sounded like something she'd say, but there wasn't your mothers usual embarrassed stammer when sex jokes in your family got too raunchy for her,

"We both saw how you were looking at her." Your mother's lips twisted further downwards.

"I-I didn't mean to!" It was your turn to look broken.

This strange assault from two unlikely sources was frying your brain.

And why wasn't anyone else in the restaurant reacting? It wasn't that big of a place and you hadn't been all that quiet so far.

When you looked around no one was even looking towards your table, conversation around you was as lively as ever. For fuck sake, there was an elderly couple right behind you, gossiping about fuck knows, but none of it sounded even remotely like you.

You just dumbly looked back at Morgan, who seemed almost back to her normal self after your embarrassment, but she still looked like a kicked puppy.

Then a thought hit you, were you being fucked with right now? It seemed elaborate beyond belief, but you didn't know this girl at all yet your mother said she did, on top of which, your mother seemed really happy when you suggested this particular diner....

"Again, I'm really sorry. Oh, right let me just get your food real quick, it's probably done."

Once Morgan departed you turned back to your mother, a little chuffed.

"What was that?"

Your mother got to it before you.

"What was what?" You scoffed back

"You obviously wanted something from her, why didn't you just go for it?"

"Go for it? Right here, in front of all these people!" You felt like your roles had been reversed.

"Why not? She was just trying to give good customer service!"

Your mother seemed passionately upset by your decision to not get blown by a barely legal stranger in full view of even more strangers. If you weren't starting to believe this was an elaborate ruse, you'd have been stunned silent.

"You know what, you're right. I was just blown away by how gorgeous she was I got scared, but seeing as how she offered, maybe I'll take her up on it."

Two could play whatever game she had concocted.

Except she didn't seem upset anymore. In fact she seemed pretty darn happy….

"H-here's your food." A breathless Morgan, back even faster than when she had collected your drinks, placed a plate in front of your mother then another in front of you, "Sorry for the wait." She then stood back up straight, smoothed out her apron, then kept her eye's on the floor.

What was this reaction? She didn't seem like she was acting, but maybe your mom had enlisted someone with some actual skill. She said this girl was Dana's classmate, but that didn't mean she actually was.

"I, umm, ha ha, I guess you want --" Morgan was playing with the hem of her dress nervously before you cut her off.

"I'd love it, but I think it'd be proper if the one offering took something off first."

You had her now. You were on to her and your mother, and you were going to push until they were forced to back out.

"Certainly." Morgan snapped to attention, her cheeks going pink "Is there anything you'd like me to take off first?"

You were hesitant for only a second, she was

committed, you'd give her that, but she opened the door for the perfect opportunity. In a dress that short…,

"How about you give me your panties."

Checkmate.

"Of course!"

Yeah right!

She reached under her dress.

She should quit now, you called her bluff. Right?

She started bending down until she touched her toes.

Hold on….

She shuffled her feet for a bit.

She isn't really….

"Oh how cute!" Your mother reached across the table and snapped up the panties from out of Morgan's outstretched hands before you could even comprehend how far this girl had gone.

… Huh?

You dumbly looked at your mother, proudly holding up a pair of lacy white panties up into the air, cooing over it and asking where the girl got them. Then back at the girl, red in the face, but answering immediately.

Come again?

No one was even looking towards your table. A cute waitress just took off her panties and your mother was holding them high in the air, turning them over in her hands, and no one cared.

"So, would you like me to take anything else off or...." Morgan trailed off, biting her lip and staring directly at your crotch.

You looked back at your mother, silently wondering what kind of girl she hired for what absolutely positively had to be a prank. Or what came over your mother to suddenly be okay with a prank like this.

"Oh, dear, I'm sorry, here." Your mother giggled to herself and reached across the table, dangling the panties by a leg hole towards you.

You silently picked them up and before you knew it were taking a deep whiff. Morgan yelped for a beat, but you hardly registered it. Her panties smelled faintly of sweat, certainly not fresh, but hardly used.

You were starting to doubt yourself, but decided to redouble your efforts to try and win this game.

"How about you bend over for me real quick, let me get a good look."

Morgan turned two shades darker, and sucked in her lips, but quickly turned on the spot then bent over, even flicking up her dress a little to make sure you got a good look.

Sure as shit, she was bare. From her pale round cheeks to her unprotected slit. You even noticed that she didn't do a heck of a lot of landscaping, just enough that any lucky guy going to town on her wouldn't get lost and need a search party to come for him.

Only now did you notice the tent you were pitching in your pants.

And as you quickly looked around, you finally noticed a few stares from some businessmen opposite you, they were smirking amongst themselves and chatting conspiratorially, but beyond that, there was no strange reactions. Even your mother was smiling while pushing

22

a slice of toast into her mouth.

"Well go on dear, your food's going to get cold if you don't hurry up." You mother waved at you.

"S-so do you still want a blowjob or…." Morgan trailed off from between her knees, at this point unsure if she was red from being upside down or some other reason.

You didn't even know how to handle this anymore so you just reached down and started to unzip your pants. If this is what they wanted, they'd damn well get it.

"Yeah sure, come on." You beckoned Morgan closer as you worked your dick through your pants.

Within a moment you were free, expecting cameras and laughter galore. Instead, Morgan crawled across the bench, and slipped her tongue across the bottom of your shaft.

Your cock twitched violently, bopping the unprepared girl on her nose, eliciting and quiet gasp from her as she tried to wrangle your bobbing member with her tongue.

A quiet clink drew your attention. It was your mother… scooping some of her scrambled eggs onto a slice of her toast. Still smiling at you when she could clearly see your dick, which was slowly entering this girls mouth.

What was even happening?

Morgan took your head into her mouth and swirled her tongue around it.

Who even cared what was happening anymore,

"This is great." You mumbled, throwing your head back and leaning against the wall.

"Thanks." Morgan popped your rod out of her mouth so she could smile up at you.

Instead of taking you back in right away, she spat into the palm of her hand and started to jerk up and down your length, making a wet slapping noise with her hand.

At the sound of the noise you had to fight back cumming right then and there. Every sensible bone in your body was screaming at you for what you were doing, it was crazy. Unfortunately, your one senseless bone was in charge right now. You were only able to muster up enough will to make sure no one was getting ready to call the cops.

Most people were still engrossed in their own conversations. Everyone except the three business men at the table across from you booth, who were all smirking at you, and your mother who was busy smiling at you while calmly finishing her meal.

You weren't exactly ecstatic with the fact you had an audience, specifically the mother part of it but you were being blown by a cute girl, so you weren't much for complaining at the moment. Instead you just muttered,

"Perverts..." Then ran an appreciative hand through Morgan's hair.

You managed to coax a bit of a purr from her as she worked her mouth up and down the first half of your cock.

You quickly reigned in your hand a little shocked by the noise, as good as it felt, it struck you that she wouldn't want her hair ruined, so you settled for petting her gently. Regardless of what you did, she was busy bobbing her head up and down in an unconcerned and steady rhythm.

"Hmm... you're right...." Your mother mumbled across

from you, in an icy voice that brought back horrible childhood memories.

You were quickly brought back to your current situation as you saw your mother push her plate away from her and slide out of the booth.

Was this game finally over? Did she hear you call her a pervert? You weren't grounded were you?

A moment later as you looked on in horror, your mother stepped over to your side of the booth, plopped down behind Morgan, and pulled her plate towards her.

Morgan was forced to press forward, sticking her ass high in the air and folded herself up like an accordion to give your mother space while still keeping your dick in her mouth

"I'll take care of this." Your mother leaned over the girl and crooned gently, lifting the girls feet onto her lap as she sat back up straight.

Your mother then tugged the girls dress down as far as she could make it and gave the three businessmen a glare that was the bane of all the fun/dangerous parts of your childhood. The men looked disgruntled and were clearly muttering amongst themselves, but they quickly turned around and went back to whatever they were doing before they started watching you.

Oh right… Morgan wasn't wearing panties anymore. And also, you were a man now, living in a dorm twenty minutes away from home, your mother couldn't ground you!

You were about to say something about the panties, but Morgan snaked a second hand forward, you hadn't noticed before, but she was probably trying to cover herself with it, but now with your mother's help Morgan had a hand to fondle your sack.

Between her new position, with her ass in the air, the fact she was pantyless and the new sensation of her gently massaging your balls you couldn't hold back anymore.

You consciously held back in an attempt to keep her styled hair intact, but you pressed down on Morgan's head and started to unload without warning. She pulled back a little, gurgling in surprise, but you kept just enough pressure on her to keep her on as you filled her mouth with your seed. You kept her there even after the last spasm, her cheeks puffed out a little as she seemed unsure of what to do with her new mouthful.

Just as you were about to give her some respite, you felt a burst of suction and her cheeks caved in and you heard a very audible gulp as her throat tensed. Your exhausted meat twitched slightly at this as you let her go and leaned back against the wall.

"That was fantastic." You muttered.

"Thank you." Morgan chirped, scooping up a stray dribble of cum that had managed to make its way down her chin back into her mouth, "Like I said, we pride ourselves on good service here!"

She didn't look red anymore, maybe a little pink and winded thanks to your big finish, but nothing like before.

"And… sorry." Now that you had a clearer head you were kind of regretting several things that had just happened.

"Oh don't be!" Morgan rubbed your arm reassuringly, "I'd have hated to have to wash up and ruin my makeup anyways."

That was actually not one of the thing's you were

apologizing for. Come to think of it though you probably should've been.

"Also, I didn't realize others could see you…." You trailed off and dangled her panties in front of her face.

"Oh, n-no problem…." Morgan started to blush again, looking away.

She was so close, what with your mother boxing her in, she was still on her hands and knees with her head above your depleted meat, you could actually feel her face start to radiate more heat. And she still wasn't grabbing her panties.

"Here you go." You awkwardly mumbled, jiggling the piece of clothing.

"Oh, right! Thanks." Morgan stammered.

"I got it." Your mother, wiping her face with a napkin and depositing it on her empty plate released Morgan's dress and with a now free had snatched up the underpants and started working the pants up Morgan's legs getting a weak repeat of the girls thanks.

Morgan for her part seemed mortified, her face growing more flushed as she refused to look anywhere but your lap.

You knew exactly how she felt right now. You couldn't even put yourself together what with her head hovering in the way.

A moment later your mother gave the girls panties a gentle snap and asserted she was done.

Morgan gave one last thanks and started fiddling with your dick again. You inhaled sharply, not prepared for a second round, but you no longer felt the cold air drying the spit from your cock and a second later heard a faint zip. Then Morgan shuffled backwards, crawling over your mother and standing back up straight.

"I hope you've enjoyed you stay so far."

You looked down and found she had zipped you back up before she left.

Of all the things that happened today… that was definitely one of them. You were busy dwelling on it, barely even registering that you mother was asking for the bill and a doggy bag for your untouched plate.

As you absentmindedly paid the bill as promised, you couldn't help but reflect on an earlier part of the

exchange, had your mother and Morgan been
expecting you to fuck her?

You drove her downtown as a favor, so regardless of your flurry of thoughts it was only right for you to drive her back. The drive back was pretty quiet. By that you mean you were quiet, your mother was busy gushing about Morgan Shenbaum. There was plenty of fluff to what your mother was saying, so you didn't need to pay much attention to get the meat of it. She was valedictorian two years in a row, going on third from the sounds of things, head of several clubs,semi-decent at a couple sports, and seemingly had a fetish for being busy since she did plenty of non-school related activities.

In no time at all you were back at the family home, cutting your mother's ramblings short.

"Oh, we're back already, well thanks sweetie, this was a fun day." Your mother, thankfully, stopped gushing about how great some random girl you literally just met was, and started getting out of the car.

"Yeah, I thought so too…." You smiled back, certainly for different reasons.

For some reason your mother was absolutely beaming.

"Uh, hey, you mind if I come in?" You stopped your

mother from closing the door, "I didn't get to eat yet, and I was maybe thinking of having a chat with Dana if she's home."

Your mother practically squealed when she agreed, waving frantically at you to follow. She was a woman in her mid forties, yet looked like she was in her late twenties, and she had a bounce in her step, just short of skipping like someone in their early teens.

If you had a clearer head, you'd have assumed something was up, but you had bigger issues right now than what got your mother so hyped.

As soon as you stepped in the front door you were swept up with a wave of nostalgia, you'd been in the entry way just this morning, a simpler time where strangers didn't blow you and your mother surely would've had some choice words if they did. You visited often enough though that it never really felt like a foreign place.

After taking off your shoes, your mother ushered you into the kitchen, where as luck would have it Dana was sitting at the table, slowly making her way through a bowl of cereal. Her straight, shoulder length platinum blonde locks a frizzy mess, and she was still wearing fuzzy pink pajamas, with barnyard animals spotting it every inches or so, like something you'd see a child wearing.

"Awe, you should've told me you were bringing something back. I wouldn't have eaten anything!" Dana pouted.

"Hand's off, it's mine. Maybe if you actually took mom shopping you'd have gotten something."

At the same time you were both pretty sure she wouldn't have been able to finish it anyways. Dana had a small body and an appetite to match. Somehow a bowl of cereal actually managed to tide her over for most of a day.

Part of your snark came from how you were a little jealous that she was just getting up at one-thirty in the afternoon, it was a weekend so to be frank, if your mom hadn't asked you to take her shopping you'd probably still be sleeping right now.

Dana stuck her tongue out at you for a moment before going back to her cereal, completely unperturbed.

"Oh Dana! Jason has something he want's to ask you!"

You and your sister both were caught off guard by this, and exchanged a look of mutual curiosity.

"Uh… yeah" You took your seat and opened your Styrofoam tray.

You took a bite of your food to try and buy time to figure out how you were going to broach the subject, when your mother spoke up again,

"We went to a diner downtown and met Morgan Shenbaum, you know, that girl from half your classes."

"Ugh, more than half." Your sister rolled her eyes.

"Is she, always so… loud?" You were hesitant, mostly because your mom was still in the room, just watching.

"Ah-yup." Dana's eye's went wide and she nodded energetically.

"And so... bubbly?" You gave your mother another sidelong glance but she seemed rooted.

"Oh god, there's being an overachiever, then there's being Morgan. Most people trying to show off their goody two shoes might feed the homeless, but Morgan would give them a sponge bath a back rub and tailor them a new wardrobe by hand if she thought it would look good on a college resume."

Since it seemed your mother wasn't going anywhere anytime soon, you just went for it,

"Does she put out?"

"Jason Thornton! That's highly inappropriate!"

"Hah! Keep dreaming! She's out of your league!" To your sister's credit she ignored your mother completely, "She actually does stuff with her free time --"

"Unlike you?" You quickly cut her off, pinching the sleeve of her pajamas.

Dana roughly yanked her arm away and scowled,

"I'm founder of my school's men, and women's gymnastics teams." Your sister pouted.

"And I'm in college." You fired back with a smirk.

Truly, on paper your sister's achievement sounded much more impressive, than just applying and being accepted somewhere, especially since she was even the unofficial advisor for both teams. The truth was though, the boy's team had some serious turnover and really only existed as a separate team because most of them only joined to ogle your sister and the other bendy girls in leotards and were being nothing but a nuisance in co-ed practices. Hell from what you've seen and been told through Dana's venting was that there were only two or three halfway decent members, the rest only joined to try and hit on Dana.

Whether Dana knew what you were thinking or not, she didn't push the issue.

"Besides, from what I've seen of her parents if they knew she even looked at a boy 'inappropriately'" Dana rolled her eye's nearly into the back of her head, and dropped her spoon to make aggressive air quotes, "no one would ever see her again."

Well that answered a lot of questions you had, but raised even more that you were pretty sure your sister couldn't help with, so you shrugged then silently started making your way through your cold meal.

After a minute of looking between you and your sister frantically, your mother finally shuffled out of the room, looking defeated.

You spent another couple hours bumming around the house, offering help where you were needed while you tried to think of what you were going to do next. There wasn't much to do around the house though, besides which Dana didn't look to be getting ready to go anywhere, so you quickly called it a day and headed back to your dorm across town giving her a chance to do something.

As soon as you entered your dorm you dropped your pants and shuffled off to your room. It was a habit you developed ever since your roommate got kicked out. It was a dry campus so when your roommate was caught with beer cans covering his room he was immediately kicked out of on campus housing. And thanks to his weak constitution and poor decision making skills he had pissed in every corner of the room, and spilled more beer than you ever drank making it uninhabitable by a replacement and even granting you a discount on your rent by the school. You basically got an entire flat to yourself for a steal, since the school was taking it's sweet time getting cleaners in.

It wasn't even five yet, but you decided to head to bed, the events of the day exhausting. Maybe if you slept on it you'd be able to sort out things when you woke up.

That was the plan anyways, but even though you fell asleep shockingly easily, it was a restless sleep. You were tossing and turning, until you woke up in a cold sweat.

When you woke up you couldn't remember what you had been dreaming about, but you found you had a raging, painful erection.

Maybe that was the problem?

You quickly went to the washroom, forgoing using porn, the memory of the earlier afternoon would suit you just fine.

You managed to rub one out in record time, which was truly impressive, considering you used to be sixteen at one point in your life. After cumming like you'd hadn't relieved yourself for a couple weeks the pain had subsided, but you didn't feel the usual afterglow of your typical orgasm. Honestly, if you had to say, you'd almost felt like you were even hornier than before.

In frustration, you stomped back to your room. You barely had time to flop onto your bed before you felt your loins stirring once again. You did everything you could think of to fight it, you flexed your thighs, you tried to think about anything but sex, you even tried to think of the old lady from the thrift shop. None of it did more than delay the inevitable. Ten minutes later you were at full mast. You just tried to ignore it, hoping it would go away by itself, but the longer you ignored it the more it started to hurt. By an hour it was starting to feel like when you've jerked a few too many times in a single day. At this rate it'd be throbbing like earlier in another hour, maybe hour-and-a-half. You planned on jerking it again, but then you remembered the earlier afternoon.

As soon as you considered actually plowing someone you were certain that would help. If you're horny and can't get off yourself, get someone else to do it. Made sense, right?

You sat up, threw on your shirt and looked for your pants.

Oh right, by the door.

You quickly grabbed your wallet off the tiny desk you had beside your bed and got your pants by the door, then practically ran to your car and peeled out of the student parking lot.

In the back of your mind you were pretty sure you hadn't taken your wallet out of your pants earlier, but that didn't matter right now, you were horny as all hell.

As you drove around you spotted an all night diner just a block away from campus.

That would work! It was a diner like before, so maybe the waitresses would act the same?

Just as you were about to pull in you managed to rein yourself in and kept going down the street.

What if they didn't act the same? Could you just ask for a blowjob? And if you did what then? What if they didn't even share the same nonchalance as the other diner? They were only a block away from your school, plenty of students visited there, you were bound to get recognized and the rumors would spread.

You drove further into town, spotting a few twenty-four seven fast food places, but you had managed to scare yourself away from those places too. In the end you wound up driving an hour out of town to a much smaller one nearby. You were significantly more comfortable out this way, especially since it was about ten at night by this time so there would hopefully be less people to recognize you even awake, let alone nearby. Though perhaps comfortable wasn't the best words since your penis was starting to throb worse than any headache or hangover you've ever had and you could barely keep your mind on anything other than slamming into a warm wet hole and coating the insides with your seed.

Eventually you spotted a neon sign down a quiet city street, point down a stairwell. There was a glowing, frothy tankard on the sign and that's all you needed to know. You were forced to park nearly a full block away since there was only street parking and it was packed, but that didn't matter.

As soon as you pulled the emergency brake and got your keys out you ran back to the neon sign as fast as your legs could carry you. You flew down the stairs and pushed open the door.

You were immediately overwhelmed by a rush of body heat, B.O. and enough fermented yeast to make you a little light headed with just a whiff. The place was nuts to butts with drunks of every shape and size. Everything from 'sad hobo' drunk, to 'sexy business woman letting her hair down and relaxing' drunk.

The place looked like a giant open basement, no chair's, just tall standing tables and a bar up against one wall. You noticed standard bar entertainment, a pool table, a couple dart boards, some TV's although they seemed to be playing whatever those nearest wanted to watch rather than sports exclusively, and against the largest wall there was a couple projectors aimed at it showing some video games were being played. All thing's considered, if it wasn't for your raging (almost literally) hard-on, you'd have been pretty taken with your lucky find. This place looked pretty chill.

"Wait right there kiddo!" A youngish looked woman with copper hair pulled into a ponytail, arms loaded with drinks commanded you, confidently strutting past you, towards a nearby table.

You couldn't help but drink her in. She was short, easily head and shoulders below you, Dana's size, but far more filled out. She had a bit of fluff that suggested she knew the menu of this place inside and out, but she carried it well. Most of her weight ended in her thighs and rear, with the rest being split between the rest of her. Her arms weren't overly flabby either, which you took note of when you were drawn to her sleeve tattoo, some sort of watery scene, with something green coiling through it.

"Alright, now could I see some I.D.?" The woman was now in front of you.

From up close you noticed that she had shaved one side of her head, leaving behind a copper fuzz. You were also able to tell that it was a dragon on her arm, bursting through some sort of body of water, it's head was drawn just above her breasts. You couldn't tell whether her low cut black tank top was an effort to show off her full tattoo or get extra tips with her asset's, probably both, but you were drawn in either way.

"Hey!" The woman snapped her fingers in your face several times, "It's a two drink minimum to stare, now I.D.!"

"You've got a nice tattoo." You stumbled out, going red in the face.

She gave a wry grimace that suggested this was far from the first time she's heard that from someone staring down her shirt. You tried to ignore her and fumbled for you wallet and flipped it open, showing your student I.D. Painfully aware of the aching tent in your pants.

"Government issued love." The woman's smile was gone.

"R-right." You fished out your driver's license and showed it to the woman.

She ended up scrutinizing it for a painfully long time, or maybe it was just your aching meat that made it feel that way. Your eagle eye view of her chest wasn't helping things either.

"Well, alright, this seems legit, anything I can get you?" The woman thrust the card back into your chest, nearly making you drop it.

You were so horny by this point you didn't even attempt to sugar coat it,

"You." You smiled awkwardly.

"How about you buy something first big boy." The woman had lost all hint of congeniality now.

Did that mean it didn't work? Or was she just making a suggestion?

You quickly scanned the menu before finding some cheap --relatively anyways -- brew and pointed it out.

You made sure to order two. You got a slight smile from her as she walked off. You wanted to appreciate her thick rear and her involuntary sway, but you couldn't. Every fibre of your being was starting to scream at you to just rip her clothes apart and plow her the second she got back. The pain in your crotch was getting nearly unbearable, but it was nothing to how horny you were. You didn't think lust could hurt, but your mind was focusing into a horny laser where the only thing you could think of was sex and it felt like your stomach would boil over if you didn't get your dick wet soon.

While you were busy trying to fight through the pain, your waitress had returned, two bottles in one hand and a bottle opener in the other. She quickly popped both caps then shoved the beers at you.

"There you go, now if you'll excuse me, I'm needed behind the bar." Without waiting she turned on her heel.

"Wait!" You called out before you even realized.

With a visible sigh the woman turned around, and looking completely unimpressed, asked you what you wanted.

You were starting to seriously consider that whatever

the fuck happened in the afternoon wasn't happening here and you'd just have to try rubbing one out again, but you came this far,

"You said two drinks would let me stare."

The woman scowled at you, crossing her arms over her cleavage and giving you a look that screamed you were starting to push your luck.

You were starting to wither, pain in your loins be damned, you weren't going to get thrown into a holding cell over it for sexual harassment.

At least that's what you kept trying to tell yourself.

"He's got you there Kari!" A loud, sweaty, beer stained drunk from a table right next to yours laughed.

He would've looked like Santa on his day off, what with the sleek bald head, and bushy white beard and jolly gut, but the copious beer stains on his wife beater and crazy look in his eye wasn't very child friendly.

"Stuff it Kurtz" Kari barked, shouting to be heard over the bustle of the packed place.

Her booming voice elicited some 'ooh's' from the

nearby tables, like a bunch of middle schoolers when a kid was called to the office over the P.A.

All the same, Kari lowered her arms from her chest and grumbled,

"That what you want?"

She was still staring daggers, but she didn't seem otherwise hostile. You decided to press your advantage,

"I think I'd like the view better without the shirt." At this point you were fighting with everything you had to not whip it out right then and there, but you had to be sure it would work like before.

"I'm sure you would." Kari's scowl deepened, and she was about to cross her arms over her chest again, but seemed to think better of it.

From less than two feet away Kurtz cupped his mouth and belted a rumbling,

"Boooooo!"

"I said fuck a donkey, Kurtz!" Kari roared right back.

"She got you good man!" Someone laughed.

You didn't know who though because right before your eyes Kari was grabbing the hem of her shirt and lifting it over her head. Without the plain black tank top, you noticed she had another giant tattoo on her side opposite her sleeve tattoo, this one was a collage of plenty of different thing's, you couldn't take it all in, mostly because they stopped short of her tits which were far more entertaining, you just knew there was a lot of fire and greenery to the body art.

"I suppose you'll want the bra next?" Kari snorted like a bull ready to charge, even as she was reaching around behind her to unhook herself.

"Yeah, because every man wants a girl to take off her shirt so he can admire her underwear." Kurtz started to laugh uproariously, his sizable gut jiggling.

You thought for sure Kari was going to go off on him again, but it seemed once her frustration hit it's peak she was reverting back to good humor. She was smiling ruefully again, her scowl softening.

"This get you going?" Kari rolled her eyes and juggled her melons.

They were pretty sizable, although you believe she had been wearing 'performance enhancing equipment.' You were in admiration of incredibly contrasted tan lines though. It looked like she favored a bikini that would've been conservative if she wasn't so meaty. Not to say it was slutty, but it looked like it could've used a bit more fabric. Over all she was a pale redhead, but her ghostly white flesh in the shape of a bikini top showed just how much paler she could get. It also made her large pink areolas all the more eye catching.

In lieu of a proper response you started to unzip and grunted,

"Blowjob."

Kari dropped her tits instantly their weight becoming incredible apparent as they less bounced and more seemed to try fruitlessly to drag her down with them. She then started to wag her finger at you, scowling deeply,

"I said two beers was good for a look, you're gonna have to buy a lot more than that --"

"Booooo!" Kurtz belted into Kari's face once again.

"Kurtz, I swear --" Kari looked ready to slug him.

"Blow him! Blow him! Blow him!" Kurtz started to chant, beating his table with his fist.

Kari took a step towards Kurtz, but a second later his tablemates joined the chant which seemed to catch her off guard. A moment later, someone else joined in from another nearby table, then another, and another, and like a wildfire in moments the entire bar of thoroughly sauced drunks was chanting in harmony,

"Blow him! Blow him! Blow him!"

Kari had gone from fuming to deflated. She hung her head and rolled her eyes up to look at you,

"I guess you're getting a deal this time." Kari mumble and bent over bringing her face within inches of your fly.

You hadn't thought to wear underwear so as soon as you unzipped entirely, the beast was unleashed, striking Kari on the nose as it bobbed up and down.

You were half a second away from grabbing her hair and thrusting in, the only thing that stopped you now was what happened next.

"I guess someone is ready to go already." Kari grinned

up at you then without missing a beat took you into her warm, wet mouth.

It was like dipping into a hot bath after spending the last ten hours at the gym. Your pain started to ebb and even your lust started to clear enough to think straight again. Enough to notice that the entire bar was now caught up in an ear splitting cacophony of cheers and laughter. People were starting to toast and pat each other on the back.

Amidst the clamor, you attempted to speak your mind,

"You've got a hell of a body."

The only sign that Kari heard was when she rolled her eyes the way only a woman with generous proportions waiting tables in a bar filled with drunks could. She probably heard similar so much that she couldn't take it as a compliment.

Kari had gone slow and messy at first, drooling all over your meat, slowly taking your entire length into her throat like a pro. She held you in her throat for a few seconds before pulling back for a breath, then she angled your cock upwards and started to go to town. She pumped half your dick with her hand and worked the rest of you with her mouth like a porn star. She was an absolute machine, pistoning her hand and head in perfect synch.

You couldn't stand up to her, and in mere minutes you started to unload into her mouth. Kari took it like a champ, not startled in the least, though she did stop bobbing once she felt the first load. She seemed fully prepared to take your load, but you had other plans. As soon as the first load struck, you grabbed a fistful of her hair and yanked her back.

Kari yelped, spitting the load you landed in her mouth out, dribbling it down her chin and onto the floor, but quickly recovered, sticking her tongue out and letting you paint her face.

Despite cumming twice today, once mere hours earlier even, 'paint' was an apt description. You coated her forehead, plastered an eye shut, and got one of her cheeks with a couple ropes. Once you stopped spraying her, Kari leaned in and milked the last few drops onto her tongue, eliciting another round of cheers.

It was like you had a full body orgasm. Your entire body felt lighter, like you'd just had a full body massage. You felt refreshed, calm, like you could finally think clearly for the first time in years. It was as if your head had been in a vice and you hadn't even noticed until you'd been set free.

"Holy shit, you got him off in no time, how about giving me a turn!" Kurtz roared, his belly bouncing as he chuckled.

"How about I call in your tab right now!" Kari stared him down with her one free eye.

"I just realized, I don't even like blowjobs." Kurtz turned around and took a deep draw from his mug.

"Well, alright then." Kari dusted her hands and looked at you, "I guess you've got what you wanted so I'll be getting back to work."

She wasn't nearly as cheerful as when you first stepped into the bar, but she seemed less disgusted by you, despite being coated with your seed.

Only problem being....

"Look again sweetheart." Kurtz had turned back around and playfully slapped Kari's bare shoulder as she reached down to grab her clothes and pointed down at your crotch.

You were slightly embarrassed at the man casually gesturing to your dick, but he had a point. Your point was still at full mast.

A murmur went through the drunken crowd and eventually someone in the back slurred loudly,

"Woo! Round two!"

And like that, a new chant was started

Kari's eye went wide and her mouth went slack for a moment,

"Alright kid, I'm kind of impressed now. You want another blow job? Or something else?"

She didn't seem to even consider the possibility that you wouldn't want to go again. Further proof how experienced she was.

You were starting to get caught up in the crowd yourself, and in a new burst of confidence stared her down and commanded,

"Take off your pants and bend over." As you spoke you

started to undo your belt as fast as you could.

"Yes sir!" Kari saluted with a smile, a somewhat humorous gesture considering she hadn't wiped off a drop of her facial yet, but something about her smile suggested she knew how she looked.

You were pretty sure she didn't hate your guts anymore. It also seemed like she was getting caught up in the crowds cheers as well, because as soon as she kicked off her panties, leaving on only a pair of beat up looking blue loafers, she did a little pirouette, making sure to stop facing away, then grabbed her ankles.

Her thighs were beautifully thick the shape of a conservative piece of underwear imprinted on her flesh. The leg holes of which were angled up sharply which suggested her ass attempted to devour her pants more times than she was willing to fish them out.

Without hesitating you sunk your fingers into her thick butt meat and slowly worked your way into her fold. She seemed to be getting turned on by the events, but the copious amount of spit she and coated your shaft with was still a lucky break for her. You had enough of her saliva coating you to start going wild from the get go.

You started pistoning in and out with fervor, which was quickly bringing some natural lubrication out of Kari. You grew flush with excitement doing a curvy waitress in front of a packed bar amidst cheers and appreciative comments.

Looking down you could see the back of Kari's head, her ponytail sweeping the floor as she fought to keep balance every time you thrust into her. You were immediately overcome with the urge to get rough with her.

Summoning up strength you didn't know you had, you pulled out, an act that drew a pall over your audience, and a surprised flick of Kari's head. You then bent over and got a look at her confusion even as she had her hands wrapped around her ankles. Then you reached between her legs, just behind and above her knees, knit your hands together behind her neck and heaved upwards.

Kari let out a high pitched curse in surprise and started flailing for something to grab onto. Her struggles weren't helping you so you had to take a few hesitant steps to keep your balance. Perhaps realizing she was doing more harm than good, Kari switched tactics and awkwardly reached one hand behind her and started pawing at you, in what might've been a weak show of resistance, all while she let out a long string of curses, which were quickly swept away by the roar from the crowd.

You wasted no time pistoning in and out of the girl like your entire life had been leading up to this one moment. Her loose fitting, casual shoes slowly being shaken off her feet as you bounced her up and down in time with your thrusts.

Despite your best efforts your strength was quickly starting to flag. Not to be rude, but the simple facts were Kari was overweight, and you were under strong. No matter how well she carried it she was probably a hundred and thirty or forty pounds. You were surprised you held her up for as long as you did.

You started walking back to the table you had claimed as your own.

"The beer!" A frantic shout cut through the crowd.

Suddenly, Kurtz bounced and jiggled past you faster than you would've ever imagined he could move, and scooped up the two bottles you had left behind. The crowd roared in laughter at his act. All the same, he was just in time for you to roughly slam Kari onto the standing table, scooting it ahead a few inches with a shrill screech and sending her shoes clattering to the ground.

"I'll take my reward now." Kurtz whispered to you, chugging one of your beers and holding on to the other as he went back to his table.

You and Kari were both red in the face and panting, but you still had life in you. Kari was lying on top of the table but was starting to push backwards towards the floor. You got her just as she was about you regain her footing again, hooking an arm under one of her legs you lifted it back onto the table then slammed back into her. You had her pinned, her toes just barely brushing against the floor below as she flailed her legs trying to get some footing every time you pressed against her and shook the table.

She was starting to pant hard now, then you heard her grunt between breaths,

"Grab my hair!"

You didn't need to be told twice. With your free hand you sunk your fingers into her silky hair around the hair band she had her ponytail bundled up with and pulled her head back.

"Yessssss!" She gurgled, her head forced towards the ceiling by your rough yank.

So she liked it rough? Well that was fine by you.

You let her hair go for a moment, getting a gasp from her that seemed tinged with disappointment, but you quickly unhooked your arm from her leg, wrapped your now free fist around her neatly bundled hair and yanked her back again. Kari didn't even attempt to take her leg off the table this time, in fact she didn't even seem to be entirely there, she was starry eyed and biting her lip, looking entirely like she was focused on something only she could see.

Then you cracked your free hand across one of her pale, jiggly cheeks. Kari was immediately brought back to earth with a shriek, accompanied by a whoop from several different people.

"Harder!" Kari commanded once the buzz settled back down a little.

You were all too happy to comply. You struck her hard, over and over. Her cheek quickly turning red. The crowd which before had been a cacophony of drunken shouts, cheers and buzzing conversation had quickly unified into a tally.

Every slap you made caused Kari's cunt to tense around you for a moment, drawing you ever closer to climax. Once the crowd reached a unified thirteen, half of Kari's ass was a deep crimson, already showing some signs of slight bruising, and her pussy clamped down on you. She started hissing, spittle raining back down on her as you kept her head yanked back,

"Ffffffffffffuug." Kari's slurred expletive deflated as fast as it came on, her body deflating just as fast.

You were in the home stretch now. You didn't even pull out before flipping her over. Kari weakly held herself up, her head thrown back, tears streaming down her cum caked face which was frozen in a look of ecstasy as she gurgled out some weak laughter.

You looked to your side and saw Kurtz leaning against his table and watching you with a grin on his face, one of your beers still untouched beside him.

"Could you, pour that over her." You panted, pointing towards the beer then Kari's chest.

"I suppose there's worse fates for a good beer." Kurtz grumbled after thinking for a moment and walking over to you and upending the drink over Kari's chest.

As Kurtz poured you started to suckle and lap up whatever you could from Kari's chest. Just as you felt her place a weak hand onto the back of your head you buried your face in between her sweaty, beer soaked bosom and your cock deep in her snatch and started to unload, and just like in some shitty fake internet story, the crowd broke into applause.

Your orgasm was almost as amazing as before, it wasn't quite as freeing as when you covered her face, but your body tingled with every jet you shot deep inside your partner, and your exhaustion from your current session was starting to ebb. By the last spurt you were barely even panting anymore. Still beat, but you felt ready to stand and walk which was more than could be said to Kari. The copper haired waitress kept herself propped up on the table with weak wobbly arms, a stream of cum leaking out of her and onto the floor, an amount that should not have been, considering how much was coating her face from your earlier session.

"Well…" Kari gulped in air, "...that was fun." She smiled at you, cracking some of the cum that had dried around the edge of her cheek, her other cheek with a drying trail of tears running down it.

You smirked back as you put on your pants and the crowd started to disperse. Reaching into your pants and pulling out your wallet, you extracted a twenty from and took a step back towards Kari, then hesitated. You pulled out a five and handed both bills to Kari. She looked a little confused.

"For the beers." You pointed to the empty bottle Kurtz had left beside her, "And a little something extra for your friendly service."

With a wave you exited the bar. The sensible part of you had returned in full with your last ejaculation and as a newly unemployed college student you ached at leaving nearly an eighty percent tip, but you did just fuck the girl. Twenty-five bucks was a small price all thing's considered.

On your way back to your car you pulled out your phone to check the time.

One A.M.

You'd been in that bar for three hours plowing that waitress, and the drunks in there had been watching nearly the entire time. And you hadn't even noticed.

With a derisive chuckle you got back in your car and prepared for the hour long drive back to your dorm, looking forward to getting into bed and hopefully figuring out just what was going on in the morning.

now.

"I'm Christina, a Havon representative, I'm here to see if there's anyone in your household interested in some of the cosmetics I have with me today."

Or maybe you could…. Even as you shook her hand you started to zone out, thinking of all the things you'd love to do to her mature body.

"Sir?" Christina's question and looked mildly concerned, drawing attention to the fact that you had been holding her hand for what was likely an uncomfortable length.

You quickly released her hand and turned your face away. You had to get your horniness in check.

"Jason! Who is it?" A call came out from the kitchen with perfect timing.

"My mother is a little busy right now, and my sister's probably still sleeping," You rolled your eyes for affect, the truth being that any other Sunday you'd probably still be sleeping yourself, "but I'm sure we'd love to hear you out if you want to step inside."

"Oh, of course!" Christina immediately looked far

happier.

You were sure she didn't normally get this far, but couldn't contain your excitement at just how far you planned on getting with her as you closed the door behind her and drank her in from behind.

Her dress was incredibly thin, and hugged her narrow hips beautifully. You took special note of her dark black panty lines when she stepped through a beam of sunlight.

You quickly led her past the kitchen, your mother halfway out of it herself,

"Hello there! Jason, who's this?" Your mother glanced down at the basket under Christina's arm then stared daggers at you, smile still firmly planted but slightly strained as she did her best to put on a friendly face.

"I'm Christina, it's nice to meet you." Christina shook your mother's hand energetically.

"I'm Erin"

Before they could get too busy you quickly ushered Christina towards the living room.

"What's she doing in my house!" Your mother hissed as quietly as she could while still being aggressive.

"She's selling cosmetics, and wants to see if we want any."

"I'm busy, I don't have time to entertain a saleswoman! And you know she's not going to leave until we buy something."

"Speaking of, can I borrow a twenty?"

Your mother blinked at you.

"You're not actually going to buy some of her over priced --"

"That's the plan." You smiled already concocting plans to change your mind last minute and return the money.

Your mother stared for a bit so you tried to press her harder,

"You know I'm good for twenty bucks. Please?"

With a sigh, your mother shook her head, then looked towards the kitchen

"You're being ripped off... let me get my purse."

You rushed into the living room, eager to deal with your erection as soon as you could. An erection which Christina who had found a spot on the couch seemed to notice quite quickly, being that it was practically at eye level as you approached her. Her smile faltered for just a second, before she hid it.

She had her hat and sunglasses off and on a table showing sleek shiny brown hair coiled up into a neat bun.

"So, Christina, when you say cosmetic's is it just make up or…?" You decided to try to kill time with small talk while you waited for your mother to return, taking a spot on the couch beside the saleswoman.

"Uh, no... no, we, um, that is, Havon boasts a wide supply of moisturizers, perfumes and hair care products, from sprays, to brushes." Christina tried to subtly creep away from you as she gave her spiel.

She smelled like a tropical fruit basket. You didn't want to wait to get you dick inside her.

"Does the moisturizer work as lube?" You were mentally kicking yourself, even as you moved to close the distance she had opened up.

Why did you say that?

"I... suppose it might?" Christina looked at you like a crazy person and much less subtly moved to the opposite end of the couch.

You were about to follow but at the last minute caught yourself. You were letting your lust get out of control, that needed to stop. You had to mentally pat yourself on the back for your self control though.

"For the butt?"

Fucking shit!

"I'm... uh, not sure how comfortable that'd be... but it would be better than nothing I suppose...." Christina laughed nervously and started to eye the hallway. Probably weighing whether or not she wanted to try and run past you and risk letting the crazy man get an attack of opportunity on her.

"Are there any other services you offer?" You tried to stop yourself, you really did, but your dick over powered you.

With someone you were pretty sure you could fuck so close you had started to turn into an animal. It hardly helped that the pain was now causing you to want to toss the lunch you just ate.

Christina, didn't seem to notice the innuendo, maybe she was naive, or just to preoccupied with her plans of escape, or maybe she was just doing a better job hiding it than she was of how uncomfortable you were making her. Someone did get it however,

"Jason Thornton! What on earth has gotten into you!" Your mother had shown up in the hallway, twenty dollar bill in hand, and looked livid.

You only slightly cared, as you sprung off the couch.

"Oh, it's fine! " Christina quickly cooed, visibly calmer with your mother in the picture, enough to attempt and take control of the situation again, no doubt certain a sale was on the line "Although, I'm just wondering…" Her eyes flicked nervously to your tenting pants "…what exactly you mean by extra services. Havon also supplies designer chocolates and some decorative soaps as well as a monthly catalogue you can subscribe to and order from directly if you'd prefer."

You definitely heard her perk up at the 'monthly catalogue' part.

Her demeanor screamed terror, but her voice was colored with nervous apprehension, which you took to mean she genuinely didn't know what you were talking about, she was just scared of the crazy guy with a raging hard on, maybe too much to fully comprehend things.

"Oh, not much, just wondering if I could fuck you with some of those creams." You winced before you even said it, but still powered through.

"Jason!" Your mother quite literally screamed at you.

But you let it roll off you, as you lunged for the cash in her hand, praying to god it fixed everything. You hated to think it, but you honestly couldn't promise that you could control yourself at this point.

Your mother shouted as the bill left her fingers, and you heard Christina choke on her spit behind you. The bill was in your hand when you turned around but nothing changed.

You fumbled for your wallet, maybe the money needed to be in it?

"I-I should go." Christina's eyes were wide and she shot to her feet, knocking some bottles free of her basket.

She wasn't stopping, what was going on.

"Jason, Thornton! I raised you better than that! What the hell is wrong with you!" Your mother screeched at you.

Christina was in such a hurry to leave that she was having trouble getting all her things back into the decorative basket she had placed them in.

You were in deep shit now, why was she leaving? Did the wallet only work on waitresses? And why the fuck were you having so much trouble getting money in a container literally designed for it?!

It was panic. You were freaking out inside, and ended up latching onto the only thought that you could,

"Hey, I'm just asking about a product, she said the moisturizer worked as lube! I assumed that it was a part of her job to make sure it fit my needs as her customer!"

Yeah, that would work right? It wasn't just your lust addled mind convincing you that this was a good excuse. You'd buy some cream, take it home, jerk off with it and clear your head and everything would be fine. No cops, no disownment, and you could figure things out later.

And then, everything shifted.

"I suppose it is part of my job." Christina froze and murmured in a hollow tone of voice.

Your mother looked dumb struck between you and the woman then,

"I… maybe, but there's certainly better ways he could've phrased it." She was still red in the face and scowling, but she was starting to calm down.

You had no idea what happened, but the change was very clear, they both went from defcon one, to a-o-kay, and that was all you needed as it felt your dick was about to explode.

You hurled your wallet and the money to the ground and rushed Christina, literally tossing her against the couch, causing her the shriek in horror.

"Don't hurt the poor woman!" Your mother yelled, some of her anger from before returning.

Not all though, so you didn't stop.

"If I'm going to be plowing her ass she's gotta be prepared for a bit of pain!" You countered angrily.

"Excuse me?" Christina gasped in horror.

Your mother huffed, but a loud beep from the kitchen caught her attention. She looked between you and the horrified Christina for a moment before shuffling off to the kitchen in a hurry.

You quickly reached under Christina's dress and grabbed her panties. She reached her arm out towards you,

"Wait a second now! You can't really be serious! My bum?" It was such a childish word for such a mature woman to scream in horror, if you weren't so horny you could've laughed.

But instead, you yanked with all your might, nearly dragging her off the couch completely in one swift pull, knocking her over backwards and avoiding her grasps while getting another shriek out of her as well as,

"Hold on! Christina was pale and started to gasp for air, "This is a bit much isn't it? I could use my hands or feet maybe?" She started to plead.

You didn't answer you just grabbed her under her arms and tossed her across the couch, onto her stomach. Then with one hand you started to hike up her dress and grabbed at a squeeze bottle from the basket with the other hand.

"Wait, please! I'm not mentally prepared for this!"

Christina was starting to hyper ventilate. You weren't the least bit concerned though, you just needed her to stop moving. You pinned an arm down behind her back and put all your weight on her, then started to work your belt as best you could with a bottle in one hand.

Out of the corner of your eye you saw some pink and gold.

"Jason! What the hell?" Your sister, golden locks a mess dressed in her pink pajamas, cell phone in hand had peeked out around a corner tentatively but once she saw you stomped out aggressively, pale and shivering.

"I'm just getting some service from the Havon lady!" You barked, drawing a line of pink cream across the length of your meat before tossing the container to the side and working it around your pole with a few frenzied strokes.

Christina all the while squealed like a pig, and bucked like a horse, kicking her legs in a panic,

"How about I use my breasts or something? You don't need to do this! I don't think I'm comfortable with this!"

"It's anal, it's not supposed to be comfortable!" You growled, grabbing her other arm, crossing them behind her back and pressing into her. A small part of you felt a bit bad about what you were going to do to her, but your dick was in charge right now.

Dana started to laugh weakly,

"Jesus, Christ, you scared the crap out of me." Dana's shoulders drooped and she turned off her phone, shuffling over to an recliner across from Christina and fell into it, "I thought someone was being raped out here." She then gave the preoccupied Christina a weak smile.

"Please, sir. Most people just test the moisturizer on some dry skin!" Christina changed tactics and tried to reason with you, either not noticing your sister, or deciding greeting her was less important.

"Haven't you ever heard the phrase 'the customer is always right?'" You sneered as you tried to line up with the struggling woman's hole.

Dana laughed,

"You're an idiot aren't you?" She flicked on the TV, "You could just use the back of your hand. This looks like way more trouble than you need to go through for some over priced cream." Dana winced immediately and muttered a quick sorry to Christina.

You couldn't tell if Christina heard, but her fight drained out of her, either thanks to your or Dana.

You didn't hesitate to line up with her asshole and start to press forward, testingly at first.

Christina yelped, her entire body tensing, but she wasn't fighting anymore.

You pushed harder, sinking in a little bit. The first inch was like somebody had finally uncorked you, your lust that was building to a breaking point was finally starting to peter out, just enough to feel like you weren't going to explode anymore.

Christina buried her face in the couch and started to

squeal into the cushions.

You started to shake your hips side to side, trying to loosen up her suffocatingly tight hole.

Christina stopped squealing, but started beating her legs against the cushions below you.

Then you went all in. Your hips meeting with a gentle pat. Your mind almost instantly clearer. The poor saleswoman pinned below you stopped struggling and panicking, instead she arched her back and yelled,

"Ahh! Fuck!" She lapsed back into some gentle sobbing for a moment before she gasped in horror, "I'm so sorry!" She looked at your sister, who was smirking at the poor woman.

"We don't give a shit." Your sister chuckled, then went back to flicking through channels.

Your head had cleared considerably, but you were still horny as all hell. Plus you reasoned that you were already balls deep, it would've been a shame to stop now.

You started to slowly rock your hips back and forth. Christina drew in a sharp breath with nearly every pull, and muttered what you were sure were curses into the couch cushions on every thrust. Before long you had to pull out to reapply your makeshift lube.

At first Christina gasped appreciatively and tried to move, but you held her firm and pressed the bottle towards inviting hole and she groaned disapprovingly before dropping her head against the couch.

This time, you dove straight back in without any concern for her comfort. Your work thus far had prepared her for re-entry. There wasn't a shriek, but there was a long muffled whine like air being let out of a balloon as Christina bit a couch cushion.

You started to rail her ass like your dick had a beef with her large intestines. At some point Dana got up and went to the kitchen.

You buried yourself deep, stopping for just a moment so you could pull up on Christina's arms like reins then moved one hand up to her throat and went back to town.

"This cream isn't that bad! How much did you say it was?" You teased her as you bent forward to suck on her neck, taking in her fragrance.

"S-seven ninety-nine for the small ones, ten ninety-nine for the large." Christina gulped hard her voice scratchy and her eyes growing wet as you grabbed her throat and pounded her like a cheap whore.

"This is a nice ass too."

"O-oh, th-thanks...." Christina let out a quite hiccup, and you felt a tear fall across your hand as you pumped her tight ass.

"Get a room why don't you!" A sarcastic scoff hacked out behind you.

"My, what's that smell?" Another more appreciative voice joined the other.

A quick look behind you revealed your sister had returned, biting delicately into a freshly baked cookie, your mother beside her, apron gone.

You pulled out from the saleswoman and sat down on the couch, dragging her up with you. Before she could even catch her breath you hiked up her dress again then brought her ass down onto your meat get a stifled grunt of pain from her.

"She asked you a question, isn't it your job to answer?"

You growled, bouncing her up and down with an increased intensity.

"Jason don't break the poor woman." Your mother was no longer angry, but she looked concerned.

"He's got a point though mom." Dana mumbled, taking a seat back in the recliner.

Your mother didn't have a reply, instead opting to take a seat on the couch you were on, however, she made sure to give you plenty of room.

"I-it's pomegranate a-and mango." Christina hiccuped in her best attempt at regaining composure.

"Oh you poor thing." Your mother sighed staring at Christina, "I apologize for my son, he's usually not this rude to sales people, I swear."

Feeling a swelling in your loins you pushed Christina forward and onto the floor. Your mother yelped a quick warning, but Christina managed to catch herself with her hand's, her ass still raised high. You buried yourself back in and went full bore on her.

"It's fine!" Christina grunted loudly after you gave her small rear end a powerful clap.

"No offense, but he's got you crying." Dana piped in.

"At least slow down a little." You mother frowned at you.

You hardly heard their blathering though, you were so close, just a few more thrusts...

"It's fine, really." Christina took a hand off the ground and wiper her face, "It's my pleasure to serve --"

You cut her off with an animal roar and started to dump your load into her.

"It's my job to provide friendly service." Christina finished with a whimper as you flooded her ass with white cream.

After another mind and body racking orgasm you fell backwards towards the couch, drawing Christina with you, keeping her corked.

With a clear head, almost as if you'd reached enlightenment, you couldn't help but remark on some of the lessons you learned today.

Your wallet needed money to work. Apparently the money didn't even need to be in your wallet to work, you just needed to come into possession of it at some point. And it seemed like you needed to fully intend to buy something before the magic took effect. You didn't claim to know how magic worked, but considering your mother looked ready to kill you before you were certain you were actually going to buy something it seemed about right, and you didn't really want to back out on that for fear of what would happen.

Come to think of it, you wondered if you had to possess money by legal means for it to work. Although you liked to think you weren't an asshole and it wouldn't ever come to that, plus if you actually had to be a paying customer to have your fun it stood to reason that it might not even work if the money wasn't technically yours... still you couldn't be sure.

"Was that all, or can I go?" Christina tried to push off you, sounding choked up.

You held her tight, and snaked a hand under the woman's dress giving her breast a squeeze and getting a yelp.

"You've had your fun, and tried out the cream plenty, sweetie, let the poor woman go." Your mother sighed.

"Seriously?" You groaned at both the older women, "You said it yourself, this stuff is a rip off. Why can't I test it thoroughly?"

Your mother recoiled and gave a worried look to Christina, horrified at being outed. You didn't stop there though, you roughly kneaded Christina's modest chest,

"And I think it's part of her job to make sure my shopping experience is as pleasant as possible, isn't that right?"

In your clearheaded, post-orgasm state you were reminded of some of the earlier conversation where Christina had admitted to having a duty and calmed down when you pressed the 'customer is always right' button.

Christina deflated, limply hanging off your dick and let out a another quiet hiccup, a tear falling from her face,

"You can tear my poor bum up as much as you want. That's what I'm here for."

You grinned at her defeat. She didn't even have to like it, she was just compelled to believe it was your right. Another interesting revelation.

That being said, with your pain and lust now dealt with, you didn't exactly need to torment her anymore.

True, you didn't need her anymore, but you had her, and you still had some time before you had to leave, so why not?

Just as you started to lift her up however, your mother let out an ear piercing screech,

"No no no no no! Not on my couch! If you make a mess young man you're cleaning it up!"

Of course! You couldn't just slam a saleswoman in her house, in front of her and your sister without her having an issue! Figures.

With a bit of effort you managed to shuffle over to the washroom with your dick still buried in the sniffling woman. By some miracle you were even able to get her over the toilet without spilling a drop of cum.

Sitting on the toilet, her makeup a mess, her mascara turning her trail of tears black, she looked up at you like a scolded child and murmured,

"Is there anything else you want from me?"

You felt a twinge of guilt, looking down at her she appeared to be a terrified woman kept at your mercy. Her voice was dull and imploring though which suggested she was merely asking a question, nothing more.

"How about you clean up the mess you helped make?" You shook your hips from side to side to give some emphasis.

"Umm, how… how do you want me to clean you?"

You rolled your eyes, now you knew she was just being willfully ignorant,

"How do you think?"

After a moment's hesitation she took a dab of soap out of the pump by the sink and with a splash of water started to stroke the length of your cock, taking special care to avoid any unpleasantness with the soap.

You sighed, partly out of frustration that you didn't see this coming by not being specific, but also in part to how pleasant it was to feel the warm, slightly rough, slender fingers of an older woman confidently working up and down your meat. A large part of the pleasure was how roughly she was treating your package, she wasn't aggressive, but she had a firm touch as she did what she could to scrub you clean.

"Is that good?" After several minutes Christina asked you gently.

You had shut your eyes and tilted your head back enjoying the sensation, even as unexpected as it was,

"Oh yeah, you've got magic fingers…" You chuckled, she had gone into handjob territory before either of you knew it.

A moment later there was the sound of tearing toilet paper and after a short delay you felt your meat being patted dry, the sound of the toilet being flushed and a gust of wind passing by. Your eyes shot open to find Christina's dress flicking out of the washroom behind her.

"Hold on!" You shouted, power walking after her.

You caught up to her in the living room gathering up her things, tossing her panties into the basket rather than putting them on. Your mother and younger sister busy watching TV cuddled up together in the recliner. They seemed unfazed by your brutal treatment of a woman's ass in plain view of them mere minutes earlier. They merely paid you the briefest of glances before returning to their show

"The cream you used was ten ninety-nine, is there anything else you want?" Christina sniffed trying her best to give you a confident stare.

"Just the cream, but you're not done yet." You were a little surprised by her sudden confidence, or rather lack of.

She had seemed broken and pliable when you had her cornered on the toilet, now she seemed near tears, eager to leave, and willing to push to get away.

"I helped you test one of my products and then cleaned you up after the following mess, what else do you want from me?"

"Look at what you did to me while cleaning up!" You gestured wildly towards your rod, which was standing to attention.

Your wild frenzied claim drew attention from your family, but your mother quickly blushed and looked away, your sister opting to wrinkle her nose and scowl instead, as if you had just tricked them into staring at your package.

"I'm not sure what that has to do with me." Christina locked eyes with you.

You stared deep into her hazel orbs, trying to figure out just what was happening with her. Her eyes were still wet, she looked ready to burst into tears at the drop of a hat, but she was being quite assertive. One thing you did notice was she was tensed up and her lower lip was quivering, she was putting on an act for some reason or another. You weren't sure what any of that really amounted to, but you were confident she didn't really have a strong will, all you had to do was demand better service and she'd fold.

"You're not sure? Your 'cleaning'" You struck air quotes and scowled, "gave me an erection, that wasn't what I asked for, but since you started it I think it's your job to finish it, don't you?"

Christina pursed her lips, you could tell she wanted to argue, but she didn't have any experience in an argument like this one, so you went for the kill,

"Or is this the best service I can hope to get from a Havon representative?" You crossed your arms and stared her down.

Christina tried her darndest to meet your glare, but she soon gave in, looking down towards your meat weakly, then with upturned doe eyes she mumbled in a defeated voice,

"What do you want me to do?"

You grew a mischievous grin and walked over to the couch,

"I think since you decided to play dumb and pretend you didn't know what I wanted before you should try again, and do it right this time!"

Christina looked like a kicked puppy as she stared at you, but after a moment she nodded gently and shuffled over you, gently lowering herself to her knees between your legs.

"Mind keeping it down?" Dana barked turning up the volume on the T.V.

You chose not to respond, but lowered your voice from an angry shout to a degrading scoff,

"See, I knew you weren't stupid. Why'd you pretend you were?"

"I didn't want to taste my own ass." Christina mumbled without a hint of any emotion.

Well, alright then. You weren't really sure what you were expecting.

"Get to work." You grunted, grabbing her surprisingly soft and silky hair and pressing down firmly on her head.

You were met with a bit of resistance but she soon opened her mouth, stuck out her tongue and let you lower her down. She certainly wasn't expecting you to jab her in the throat though. As you kept pushing she tensed but you kept up the pressure until you buried yourself in her throat and she started to gag. You held her there for a minute as she struggled weakly. She seemed to be doing her best to deal with the intrusion and lack of oxygen, but she was quickly beginning to lose her resolve as her throat convulsed around your cock in an attempt to dislodge the intrusion.

You were having fun keeping her down, but her fingers started to dig into your thighs and she started to put up a quite a bit of fight to be let up. The second you let go she sprung backwards and gasped for air. To her credit she only drew back enough to breathe, her every warm, wet breath enveloping your spit drenched cock.

You heard a tut off to the side that drew your attention.

Still cuddled up together, your mother looked down at Christina with concern, and your sister with a frown on her face made sure to lock eyes with you before rolling her eyes halfway into the back of her head.

A moment later you felt Christina's soft wet lips take you in again. Seeing she was fine, your mother and sister turned back to the T.V.

Christina was no expert when it came to blowjobs, unable to willingly deepthroat you, but it was quickly apparent that with age came experience. She kept a tight seal with her lips and had a deft tongue. Every bob came with a delicate flick of her tongue.

You leaned back into the couch, pawing through Christina's soft hair with a satisfied groan. The only dissatisfaction you had was her hair was pulled back into a tight bun leaving little volume for you to run your hands through.

"How about we deal with this." You mumbled to no one in particular, and started picking at some bobby pins holding the bun in place.

Christina didn't answer, the only sign that she heard was that she slowed her bobbing and upped the suction and amount of tongue she was using.

After a dozen pins with change you had her hair set free, revealing a shiny, wavy shock of hair that reached down between her shoulder blades.

Without the stiff bun in the way you ran both your hands through her silky smooth hair, enjoying the feel of it around your fingers as well as the feeling below your fingers, as she slowly increased her tempo.

With a satisfied groan you grinned at your plaything and decided to taunt her a little bit,

"You're real good at this. You practice on your husband a lot?"

Christina stopped halfway down your shaft, pausing for a moment before shaking her head gently, keeping certain not to let you out of her mouth.

Not exactly what you were expecting but you could work with that.

"Oh my! You've got such magnificent hair." Your mother commented before you could say another word.

And just like that, the suction around your cock

disappeared and was replaced by short, quick gasps for air.

You were caught off guard to say the least, not because of the change in sensation, but because it quickly devolved into full on bawling.

"Jason! What the fuck!" Your sister sat up in her chair and glared at you.

"N-no, I'm sowwy!" Christina choked out, your dick still halfway in her mouth as she shook her head from side to side.

Your mother shot Dana a glare at the curse, but quickly walked over and knelt down beside the woman to rub her back.

"I'm sorry, I-I shouldn't be falling apart I-like this while I still have a job to do." Christina gasped, pulling away from your dick to speak, replacing her mouth with a limp handjob, tears cutting through her dried and streaked mascara.

You wanted to say you were horrified to have your mother kneeling so close to your exposed, spit soaked rod while she wrapped her arm around another woman who was stroking you off. You wanted to just jump up and back away. Instead, your cock twitched, and started to throb almost painfully in excitement.

"Oh, don't you worry about that!" Your mother's maternal instincts kicked in, despite the woman being very close to her own age, if not slightly older, "Jason you don't mind, right?" She asked in a tone that suggested you didn't have a choice. Her face turning to look up at you from between your legs.

You just stared at her dumbly. Her soft pink lips barely a foot away from your meat. Christina even had you angled back towards her own face. You hated to admit it to yourself, but the scene before you had you nearly ready to burst. If you just got a few more strokes, maybe you could get them both. How would your mother react…?

Unfortunately Christina seemed to take your silence as consent to stop pleasuring you and allowed your mother to lead her over to the couch beside you. The reality of the situation finally sunk in, you *wanted* to coat your mother's face, and while you felt like you should've been disgusted, you mostly felt incredibly disappointed and sexually frustrated.

"I-it's just… you all keep complimenting me and…"

Christina couldn't finish her sentence, instead bursting into tears.

"Jason!" Your sister took pleasure in shouting at you.

'You all' included her, but you somehow doubted she cared enough for you to bring that up, besides which you were probably the biggest perpetrator. Besides which, complimenting wasn't really a bad thing as far as you knew….

Your mother immediately started trying to pry into what got the woman in her state, reminding you of moments in your childhood when you'd been bullied and refused to open up. As it turned out Christina's situation wasn't entirely far off from that.

You soon learned of a relatively recent divorce from an abusive sack of trash who really bagged her on her appearance, followed closely by her incredibly recent termination of a job she's had ever since she got her cosmetology license twenty odd years earlier. Christina seemed certain, and from the information she gave so did you, your mother and sister, that it was due to the new owners of the shop thinking she was 'too old' for their image. Of course they tried to sugar coat it.

All you could do was awkwardly smile sympathetically beside the full with your still spit soaked hard on out while your mother handed her tissues and patted her back.

All you had needed was another thirty seconds, and you could've burst all over both their faces! Wait, No!

You had to get rid of these thoughts, it was just the lust talking. You just needed to cum and you'd be back to your normal self.

You were just deciding your next action when your sister roughly pushed you off the couch so she could sit beside the hiccuping saleswoman.

Your sister wasn't comfortable with a strange woman sobbing out of the blue, but she lived for the chance to give her girl-friends ego boosts while shitting on anybody who wronged them. It quickly became apparent that as far as your sister was concerned this woman was just as deserving of her input as her friends. Or rather, she got wet at the mere thought of trash talking people that deserved it. Hell, even your mother started to join in on the catty shit talking, leaving you, standing there naked from the waist down as the third wheel.

This is bullshit! You thought to yourself, crossing your arms in your mind as your family managed to coax a weak chuckle from the woman.

You couldn't take it anymore. You dropped your goofy sympathetic smile and stood over Christina.

"Jason...." Your mom started disapprovingly.

"Yeah, fuck off, can't you read the room!" Your sister finished.

"Don't mind me, I'm just getting my money's worth." You defended yourself firmly.

Your mother and sister both looked ready to jump to this woman's defence but she quickly put up a hand,

"No, he's right, I appreciate what you're doing for me, but I've been unprofessional." Christina spoke like she was going to get back to work on you, but your family quickly steered her back into venting while they sprinkled in their thoughts on whatever was coming up.

Just like old friends that would end up trying to end a conversation for three straight hours. It didn't matter to you though. Granted, her mouth would probably earn you some lip from your family, but there were tons of ways to get off with an attractive woman.

You started to remove Christina's long sundress, which got a bit of a huff from your mother and sister, but Christina was too engrossed in dishing with them to pay you any more mind than to hover out of her seat and lift her arms so you could get it off her. Seemingly taking their cue from her, your mother and sister decided to keep their mouths shut on the matter.

You were pleased to find she wasn't wearing a bra. You suspected as much when you groped her earlier, but it was always nice to have suspicions like that one confirmed.

"Well I think that's grounds for taking them to the labor board." Your mother tutted.

"Absolutely!" Dana chirped in agreement.

And sandwiched between the two, nodding her head slowly was the nearly naked Christina, the only garment left was a pair of minimalistic sandals. Then there was you... slowly bringing your head down toward her chest and then taking one of her perky little nipples into your mouth. Christina's only reaction to you was a little gasp,

"Ooh! W-well, my daughter said as much, but I'm still very close with her mother. She's the one that gave me my job there." Christina dabbed her eyes with a tissue, paying you little mind as she continued to gossip.

You took her other breast into your hand, massaging the soft flesh and rolling her nipple between your fingers as you sucked on the other one. Both nipples became erect in short order.

"What did you do there?" Dana asked with genuine interest.

You spit out Christina's nipple with a satisfying pop and were pleased to find both were erect, so you gave the both a couple playful flicks.

"M-mostly I specialized i-in hair. Guuhh." Christina stammered and groaned trying to focus on the conversation, "Styling, d-dyeing so on. b-but I did some s-skin care."

Satisfied with her chest you lowered a hand between her legs to rub the side of your hand against her fold, but were surprised with how moist she was, she was nearly ready to go already.

"Did you do manicure's? Because your nails or lovely!"

Your mother chirped.

You stuck out your thumb and roughly brushed it side to side over Christina's clit.

"Ooop! Th-thank you!" Christina gasped at a particularly high volume.

You weren't entirely sure if it was directed at you or your mother.

"I-I-I had t-training for mani's a-and p-pedi's b-but there were other g-girls to specialize in... oooh." Christina couldn't finish her sentence when you stuck a couple fingers into her fold and started to root around, running up the slick, silky sides of her cunt.

Although she gave you an idea.

"I'd love it if you could do me some time!" Your mother cooed.

You nearly jumped out of your skin until you saw she had grabbed Christina's hands and started to admire her nails.

You pulled your fingers out of the woman and brought them up to her mouth. Under her makeup it was hard to tell if she was actually blushing, but she was breathing hard. Her eye's were still wet, the tears never fully stopping, but she looked up you with apprehension for only a second before she let you put the fingers you had soaked with her own juices into her mouth and she sucked them clean with earnest.

"I'd love nails like this too!" Dana agreed with your mother, grabbing Christina's other hand.

"You and whose money?" You scoffed, drawing your fingers from Christina's mouth, a bridge of saliva following part way out before snapping off.

You then bent down and undid Christina's sandals.

Dana scowled, and without releasing Christina's hand reached forward and jabbed you in the side of the head with her big toe.

She didn't have a counter argument because she'd been through nine different jobs in the last two years because she couldn't handle difficult customers.

Tossing her sandals to the side you grabbed Christina's ankles and brought her knees up to her chest, pointing her toes towards you and pushing her feet together, you yourself remarked,

"I've gotta say though, these toes look delicious."

"Oh, thank you." Christina beamed, knocking loose a mounting tear, but from the looks of things there wasn't another queued up anymore.

As she gave thanks, you in your own way gave your own, then stuck her big toes in your mouth. Running your tongue all around them. The undersides of her feet had gotten a bit sweaty in her sandals upping the saltiness subtly.

"And you know that's a compliment coming from him." Dana rolled her eye's and let go of Christina's hand, "He's one of those guys that thinks with his dick, unfortunately. But it makes a good divining rod for what's attractive I suppose."

"Dana...." Your mother softly groaned, frowning at your sister and flicking her eye's over to the present guest... but not defending you.

Ouch. As you ran your tongue up the soft, salty soles of the beaming saleswoman in front of you were pretty hurt. Your sister was one thing, but your mother thinking that the same of you struck hard.

You pulled away from Christina's feet, and lowered

them down to your waist.

Christina was folded up against the back of the couch, and you honestly thought it looked uncomfortable, but she just smiled at you through misty eyes as you squeezed her feet together and slipped between the makeshift pussy and slowly worked your way back and forth.

Her feet were a little cold despite the warmth of the living room, but they were soft and smooth that really showed how much care she took of them despite her age and the fact that she worked on her feet.

"See." Dana scoffed with a gentle chuckle.

You only response was to let out a groan, mostly in satisfaction. Proving your sister right kind of hurt though.

As conversation moved onto a different subject you lowered the mature woman's feet and grabbed her by her tight, slender calves and yanked her down the couch a little bit so you could better line up with her now drenched hole.

"Who does you makeup by that way?" On a whim you decided to join the conversation as you sunk into

Christina, her warm hole enveloping your cock in a damp hug prompting a happy sigh from the older woman.

Immediately your mother coughed and your sister glared daggers. Christina though gave a nervous laugh and looked down between her legs,

"It's awful I know, I tried to use my daughter's thing's but I'm not very good at more than a bit of lipstick and mascara."

It was your sister's turned to cough awkwardly while your mother placed a hand on Christina's shoulder,

"It's not bad, it's just…."

"A little much." Your sister weakly tried to come to your mother's rescue.

Fully engrossed in pumping your hips you hardly registered what either said though, instead absentmindedly muttering,

"Well if this is what horrible make up looks like you must've had a lot to work with to still look this good…." Make up really wasn't your thing, you knew it could make even ugly girls hot, and they used it for some crazy detailed costumes in movies, but you were certain you'd never have the eye for it any of the women in your family did.

Out of the corner of your eye you saw your mother beaming. Christina's body shook a little which you soon found was her giggling, your sister though,

"You got a thing for older women now?" Dana wrinkled her nose at you, but was smiling nonetheless.

"Well I'm not looking for anything serious, but if Christina is interested in an occasional booty call I've got no complaints."

"Did not need to know that." Dana groaned.

Your mother responded with a half cough half chuckle.

Without missing a beat, Christina, grinning from ear to ear, locked her ankles behind you and threw her arms around your neck,

"Oh look at me, acting like a complete train wreck in a customer's house needing them to cheer me up! I've got a job to do!" Even as she was talking she started to grind against you.

Your mother and sister didn't seem to have anything else to say after that. Your mother looked proud of you as you went to town on this woman, and your sister, while she tried to avoid looking, being a high school senior and too cool to love her family, the smile on her face said it all though.

"Oh, how about I make us all some tea!" Your mother got to her feet and started shuffling to the kitchen.

"N-no, I can't intrude any... any...." Christina train of thought ground to a halt as you started picking up speed, her face started to contort into a what looked like a sneeze that wouldn't come

"Nonsense! We've really enjoyed your company." Your mother paid no mind to her protests or how they were cut short.

A moment passed and the wet walls around your meat started to contract and Christina's eyes fluttered, prompting you to let loose.

"We thought that was obvious." You chuckled with a gasp like a fish out of water as your entire body tingled with every burst you shot deep into the woman. Your pain and general soreness from last night's affairs nearly melting away entirely.

"You can just pay us back with a mani-pedi when you're feeling better." Your sister laughed herself, unceremoniously threading her slender frame between you and Christina to grab the box of tissues your mother had left on the other side of the saleswoman. "I wouldn't mind having hair like yours either." Your sister looked longingly at Christina's head, as she pulled out a fistful of tissues.

Her own hair a frazzled mess, only in part due to her bed head.

"Don't be greedy, that's rude." Playing the part of older brother you felt it was your job to try and correct your sister as you stood back up straight.

"W-wow!" Christina gasped going limp. "I-it's been years since I... s-since anyone... well...." Christina started to stumble over her words as she realized what she was saying in front of you and quickly snatched up the handful of tissues from your sister, using them to stem the tide of cum that you had let loose when you uncorked from her. "Wh-what I mean is, I absolutely do not mind. You've all done more for me than I had any right to ask." She was breathless and looked ashamed, but had a hard time hiding a smile.

"I just bought some cream and got some stellar service to boot, I'm not sure what you're talking about." You mumbled, throwing your pants back on and grabbing your wallet.

Christina looked away in an attempt to hide her full blown grin.

"Change for a twenty?" You asked, presenting the bill sandwiched between two outstretched fingers.

"Of course!" Christina perked up at the change of subject and started to throw on her clothes, "It's in my car." She started to shuffle towards the door before freezing and shuffling back, "May I use your washroom?" She leaned in and whispered.

You and your younger sister both stifled a chuckle and nodded.

"You know where it is, right?" You grinned.

Christina went off to the washroom and in relatively short order came back out with most of her makeup washed off and headed for the door. It was with great pleasure you noted her panties were still sitting within the basket of goods she had left on the coffee table.

"Where'd Christina go?" You mother frowned carrying a tray of drinks.

After a quick explanation your mother perked up and remarked on getting cookies before heading back into the kitchen.

Almost as soon as she left the room a new face popped in,

"So I just passed some strange woman leaving the house grinning like an idiot." Caitlin, your older sister had let herself in and looked quite pleased with herself.

Dana immediately started cluing her into recent event's, making extra sure to paint you in the foulest light she could, a grin plastered on her face the whole time.

Caitlin in addition to being your big sister was also the source for a horrible school life all throughout middle school up until you went to college. Not for anything she did specifically, just… hormonal teenaged boy's weren't exactly known for clear thinking. Many a jealous boys gave you shit for getting to live under the same roof as her.

Not to be weird but you kind of understood their feelings. She developed early and developed well. She probably had the best (subjectively) figure out of all the women in your house. Dana was a stick, your mother had a decent chest and a better ass, but Caitlin was blessed with an hourglass figure and a penchant for athletics that only helped maintain and define her body. It even spurred her into finding a job in personal training while she was still in her senior year of high school.

Right now she was standing in the living room, her long blonde hair tied back in a ponytail, beat up running shoes on her feet. She had on tight tank top drenched in sweat and spandex shorts hugging her tight ass. She liked to brag that the outfit had customers lining up just to train with her. While you could definitely see that happening, you kind of had doubts, given how often she was trying to pressure you into becoming a client, despite how you were broke most of the time.

If you did shell out some cash to train with her though you'd get to see her bend and lift in those tight clothing for at least an hour…. Your pants starting to tighten just looking at her in what was practically sweat soaked underwear, and the thoughts of how they got that way.

No! Gross! She was your sister!

At least that was your mantra as you tried to calm the beast in your pants. You weren't sure how your sisters would appreciate getting a look at it now that Christina was gone.

Wasn't cumming supposed to help you get rid of these thoughts? Or were you just a freak and only now realizing it?

Caught up to speed and giving you plenty of shit beside Dana, your elder sister took a spot on the couch and grabbed a cup of tea from the tray just as your mother came back in with some cookies pleasantly surprised at the new guest, quickly offering to get you a new cup of tea.

Of course the missing tea was your's and not, say Dana's. You doubted your mother meant anything by it but you still couldn't help roll your eyes at the assumption and refused. She always liked to take the side of her two little princesses….

The biggest reason you refused though was that you still had things to do today, and after a quick look at the clock realized you didn't have a heck of a lot of time left.

You bid farewell to your family and headed for the door. You got your change from Christina along the way who seemed a little disappointed when you explained you had to go, but she nodded and headed back into the living room.

That was an interesting reaction… she didn't seem at all resentful of the way you took her ass earlier…. There was still so much you didn't know about your wallet. You'd definitely have to experiment more. Your meat began to rise at the very idea.

Still, it seemed to work off money, which you didn't have any on you right now, and very little in general. That'd also need to be addressed.

Before anything else could be done you had to deal with your immediate lack of funds. It was to you luck that your bank was the only one in the entire city that was opened on Sundays. There were plenty of issues with your bank, but this wasn't one of them. Right now, you needed replacement credit and debit cards and could get some cash while you were in there.

The whole drive across town you couldn't get the image of your svelte, sweaty sister out of your head. In the privacy of your own car, much as you wanted to hate yourself for it, you couldn't help but fantasize about her. What if you took her up on her offer to hire her as your personal trainer? Would she serve you with a smile, or would you have to take her like Christina? Would she resent you afterwards if you did? Or would she being oddly happy afterwards? There seemed to be a streak of that so far. Was that just a coincidence? You technically were having sex, if you were good enough would it help convince people to view you in a better light, or was your wallet casting more magic behind the scenes? Did other people even see it even remotely close to the same way you did?

By the time you were pulling into your bank you were

starting to have an uncomfortable amount of lust. Your heart dropped into your stomach at the mere thought of feeling like a rabid badger had given you a blowjob, a sensation that was likely to follow. You had just unloaded, multiple times, not even half an hour earlier. But you were still weren't interested in feeling the hurt.

That thought quickly sobered you up and you rushed into the bank, hoping to get thing's over with quickly. You could worry about your dirty thoughts about your sister later.

As your luck would have it, the bank was empty. You sauntered up to the counter and smiled at the rather bored looking secretary.

"Oh! Mr. Thornton, how can I help you!" The woman behind the counter perked up almost immediately.

You knew her quite well since you often had to come in to withdraw cash. Given the bank's small presence in town there wasn't a very wide variety of clients and thus regulars were quite well known and you knew all the staff by name and they you.

"Yeah, I think my cards have crapped out on me and was looking for replacements." You chuckled, placing both credit and debit on the desk, both provided by the bank.

"My, at the same time? How lucky for you." The woman tutted and shook her head.

You shared a laugh.

Looking at the woman, you were seriously considering taking her right now, but you didn't have any money… and she didn't have anything to purchase.

"Now, I have to warn you, it's a twenty dollar replacement fee…" The secretary winced, as she got you to run the cards to confirm they wouldn't read, "each." She added with a sympathetic glance.

Your eyes nearly bugged clear out of your head. Sex no longer on your mind. That was highway robbery! It had to be! You weren't going to take this!

"I hate to be that guy, but is Derek in?" You were calling for her manager with a good natured laugh, despite the inner turmoil you were feeling at being squeezed like that.

"I'm afraid he left town rather suddenly a little over a week ago now." She gave you a pained smile.

You were surprised by this, left out of the loop in an institution where you were on good terms with everyone. Or you *thought* you were, but this fee had to be extortion.

"I can get you his temporary replacement though." The woman's tone suggested that wasn't going to help.

You knew it probably wouldn't, Derek was a friend, he might've been able to swing something for you, this new person though, was… new.

The secretary disappeared somewhere inside the bank, leaving you alone in the sleepy lobby, until the new manager stepped out.

Fuck Derek! was all you could think.

The new temp manager was a tall woman, with a sandy-brown complexion. South Indian you guessed. She had slender frame of a bollywood actress, angular western features, and the tits of a porn star. You almost didn't notice the angular pink gold glasses, glittering nose stud, or garishly large hair bun bordering on bee-hive, stuck in place with what appeared to be solid black chopsticks. In your defence of the last part, the chopsticks camouflaged in with her slick raven hair almost perfectly.

Getting a good look at her though, she actually looked like she could've walked out of a vintage porno playing a librarian. From her plush burgundy lips, right down to her tight black pencil skirt ending just above her knees showing off her black stockings, that hugged her slender thighs and powerful looking calfs. Granted it might've been her slutty black six inch stilettos that made them pop as much as they did. Pulling her whole look together was a half unbuttoned suit blouse showing off a plain white undershirt stretched to it's limit over her ample chest.

"Hello there! I'm Nalini, current branch manager, I understand there's some kind of problem?" She sauntered up to the counter, one practiced foot in front of the other, giving her a sway of her hips and a gentle bounce to her chest.

Despite her exotic name she spoke flawless english, it was mildly disappointing, but after drinking her in you were thinking you could forgive her.

"Yeah, uh, names Jason, I've got, these um, cards, they're broken and I have to pay to replace them?" You started stumbling over your words as you dumbly shook her hand, as your urge to stick your meat between her ripe sweater meat was rising.

"I'm afraid so." Nalini gave a sympathetic smile.

"There's nothing you can do?" The confirmation that you'd be out a generous sum helped bring you back to your senses.

"I'm afraid there's nothing we can do about the fee, it's set by head office, but if there's anything we can do to make your experience today hurt just a little less we'll be happy to do it."

What the hell did that even mean? If she couldn't waive a fee, then you seriously doubted she could do anything else that didn't cost money! And what kind of bank would charge customers so fucking much just to use their own god damn...! Hold up....

You were about to give her a piece of your mind at the empty promise, but a thought occurred. You'd be paying for a service if this went through, right? So was she saying what you thought she was? Would that even work though? The money would be taken right out of your account, it was all just numbers in a computer right now. Not a cent would come anywhere near your magic wallet. Although… magic.

"And what do you mean by hurt less?" You re-adjusted your pants behind the counter, and cocked an eyebrow at her, already starting to go wild in anticipation.

"Just what I mean sir. Here at this institution we take pride in making our customer's happy."

Goddamnit, even if she didn't have an exotic accent, hearing her talk like that was still hot as hell. Maybe a part of it was you projecting meaning onto her words, but still….

"Are you offering to go out with me?" You tried to test the waters with a grin, fighting through the urge to jump the counter and take her right there.

"I'm afraid not sir." She chuckled seductively, or at least, you were being seduced "I'm happily engaged."

Well damn, guess it didn't work if the money wasn't physical.

"Of course if you need a bit of help with your… ah, current situation. I'd be more than happy if I could be of service."

Shit she noticed you readjusting your pants! ….Wait… hold on, you've got this… you were horny as hell, not stupid.

Staring at her beaming customer service smile it took you a second to fully comprehend her, you've still only had the wallet for a day and a half now you were a little caught off guard by her brashness. Only one experience so far was anything like this one.

"That would be lovely thanks." You smiled back.

"Would you like to get the business out of the way first, or afterwards?" She reached tentatively towards your cards and spoke like letting you rail her for doing business with her was the most normal thing in the world.

"After." You groaned almost automatically, "Wait!" Then a thought struck you, "I've got some other things I need to do today so I can't spend all day here, would you be willing to take care of me along the way?" On a whim you decided to test just what your new found situation would let you do with her.

Her smile didn't waver for a second, though she took a spell to consider it. It must've only been a couple seconds, but as far as you were concerned it may as well have been an hour.

"If that's how I can best serve you, of course."

With your meat threatening to bore a hole through your pants you tried to get your business out of the way as soon as you could. You got a replacement debit card in short order and used it to withdraw a decent amount of money that should get you through the week with a bit extra to pay back your mother.

"Alright, so then, you should be getting your credit card in about one or two weeks at the provided address. Was there anything else I could help you with?" Nalini flashed a smile.

"Not with my account." You grunted.

"Of course sir, let me just gather a few things and I'll be right out with you." With her ever present customer service grin, the top heavy Indian sauntered towards the back room.

You were left alone in complete silence, but when you strained hard you could make out most of a conversation,

135

"...Yeah I've gotta take care of this guy that junked his cards. If he doesn't let me go before closing just lock up and drop the keys off at that address...."

You weren't sure you liked her tone, or at least what you could make out of it, even if she wasn't saying anything particularly rude, but you considered that maybe it was just projection. You were starting to notice that when you got painfully horny you got a bit crabby. You needed to work on that. But the really attention grabbing part was the last bit....

"Sorry about the wait!" Nalini came back into view, carrying a sleek black purse with a spaghetti strap slung over her shoulder, "Now, how can I be of service?" Her customer service smile was back, none of the bored irritation you picked up on when she thought you couldn't hear.

Looking her up and down you didn't know where to begin. She had great lips that looked like they'd be amazing wrapped around your cock. She had both hand on the strap of her purse, one arm pulled across her body and pushing up her already impressive breasts even more enticingly.

God! Was she doing that on purpose?

And while her butt was small, the way her tight skirt hugged it proved that it had some merit to it as well.

"Sir?" Nalini looked a bit concerned after a minute of you staring, "I thought you wanted to take me home, has that changed?"

"Not quite." You growled, her words lighting a fire deep inside your pants, "Take off your shirt!" You roared, yanking your zipper down forcefully.

"Of course sir." Nalini didn't even flinch as you yelled at her, her fake smile back as she gently lowered her purse onto a nearby desk for filling out forms and started to unbutton her shirt. After opening the buttons that weren't already undone, she delicately slide one sleeve off... then the other.

She was taking way too long.

As soon as her dress shirt was off you weren't able to wait anymore and roughly grabbed the collar of her cheap looking tank top and yanked. Nalini's smile faltered slightly as she yelped in surprise and stumbled towards you, the fabric giving away as easily as it looked it would.

"I-if you told me I wasn't fast enough I could've sped

things up." She grimaced slightly at the destroyed garment on the ground as she quickly shrugged off a bra that matched her lipstick in shade.

You took minor note of the tiny bit of irritation that started to seep into her voice, then locked lips with her and started kneading one of her heavy breasts.

Nalini stiffened slightly at the sudden tongue wrestling match, but like a good representative of a rather large and prestigious bank she quickly melted into it and started to kiss you back, placing one hand on your cheek and running the other through your hair the way she surely did with her fiancé when things were getting hot and heavy.

She tasted too good to break away and yet you needed release. You started to grind up against her in an attempt at relieving some of the pressure. Her eye's fluttered open momentarily then her hand left her cheek and went down, you felt it brush up against your cock and tensed. A moment later your cock was enveloped completely in a warm embrace, only a moment later her hand was back on your cheek and her kissing doubled in intensity. It was mind blowing, and yet, you were curious about the sensation, it wasn't wet, yet you felt something silky caress the top side of your cock.

You tried to break away from her to get a look but immediately had a pair of soft, forceful hands pulled you back into her sizable chest,

"Shh shh shh. It's just my thighs. Don't you worry about a thing, just enjoy yourself. I'll take good care of you." Nalini cooed like a mother scolding a child, only her voice had taken on a husky, sensual bite that wasn't present when you were talking with her before.

You weren't exactly *worried* about what a soft warm feeling around your cock was, especially not while you were making out with a gorgeous woman, but who were you to ignore an order like that?

You started move your hips back and forth slowly, breathing in Nalini's sweet scent, as she stroked your hair almost lovingly, her soft chest threatening to drown you. In response to your movements she started to flex and wiggle her thighs slightly while taking care not to dislodge you from your current position.

Without warning you drew back from your position slightly and immediately pulled one of her dark brown nipples into your mouth. She froze and gasped as soon as you did.

You looked up at her face, pinching her nipple lightly between your teeth and pulling back a little prompting a deeper gasp, her cheeks growing flush.

"You've got a sensitive chest, huh?" You grinned at her mischievously, letting her nipple free to settle back against her breast.

"Very…." She smiled back, letting out a quiet sigh.

It was hard to tell whether she was just saying that for your sake or it was the truth, going by her blush however, she was certainly feeling something.

"How about you suck on your other breast for me?" You phrased it as a request but barked it as an order, immediately taking her tit back into your mouth and thrusting between her legs with a bit more force.

"With pleasure, sir." Nalini purred back and lifted one of her large breasts up to her own mouth.

After a minute of thrusting between her soft thighs, just above her panty hose's reach you felt a dampness caressing the top of your cock. Combined with her breast in your mouth, your tongue slapping around her hard nipple and the show she was giving you inches away from your face you were soon ready to burst.

140

"Get on your knees!" You breathlessly ordered.

"Yes sir!" Spitting out her own other breast with a satisfying smack of her lips, spit trailing after and an erect nipple to match the one you gave her, she quickly got on her knees and smiled up at you.

As you started to stroke your meat over her face she opened her mouth wide and cupped her breasts together.

Your entire body shuddered and your first load launched across her cheek, prompting a flinch, but after some calibrations the rest made it into her waiting hole. Load after load until her mouth was nearly overflowing. Once you squeezed out the last drop into her mouth she pulled her lips together, her cheeks puffed out and with an audible gulp and slight shudder she opened her mouth up again to rake the errant load off her cheek and into her mouth. Then without a word she took you into her mouth, making sure she got any drop that might've been left behind.

"All gone!" She beamed up at you, after pulling off your still hard shaft.

Dammit, you couldn't afford cocaine but you assumed

this is what it felt like. You were a fiery ball of energy, but you were still barely satisfied. Just looking down at the girl staring up at you with big wet eyes, and a huge fake grin on her face, her heavy chest in full view, her tight skirt hiked up, her powerful calves in tight black, transparent fabric… you were ready to go again with a horny fury.

But just because you wanted to didn't mean you could spend all your time having sex, you had more to do today.

"Was that everything?" Nalini asked, even as she eyed your still hard shaft, bobbing inches from her face.

"No." You groaned putting your pants back on.

You hated to do it, but even with your luck at finding a magic sex granting wallet, you had other aspects of life to live, such as food. A gurgling in your stomach alerted you to just how much effort it was to pound two women in a row. The sandwich you had earlier leaving you wanting for more.

"Put your clothes on, I've got other business to deal with first."

"Of course sir."

You gave her just enough time to put on her bra, and slip her arms into the sleeves of her still intact dress shirt before you gather up her purse and tattered tank top then threw her over your shoulder.

Nalini gasped a little at the treatment but quickly melted into giggles as you stomped off towards the exit. You liked that sound, it didn't seem nearly as fake as her smile had.

As you strode out of the bank and towards your car you were starting to regret carrying the well endowed bank manager the entire way. You liked the animal feel of just taking a woman and stalking off with her, but your body liked to remind you that you hadn't trained to lift a hundred pound human being and walk around with them, and just with how top heavy Nalini was you somehow doubted she was as light as an even hundred.

As you got to your cheap junker and lowered your catch to the ground, taking care to make sure she didn't lose her balance on her high heels before you let her go.

You found that even if your body was screaming at you to give it a break, you still had the mountain of energy you had when you filled her mouth. What's more, you still had a raging need to get off packed in your pants.

"Thanks" Nalini gave you a genuine smile for once, not her over the top customer service grin, as she held her shirt closed over her bare chest with one hand using her other to hold onto you to find her balance.

It was with some trepidation you started to consider taking up your older sister on her offer to be your personal trainer. Your bank account would hate you for disembowelling it like that, and you still felt kind of horrible at the thoughts you had about her, but you were realizing you weren't in perfect shape, and there could be a lot of fun accompanied with getting into shape.

You decided to leave the thought for anther time as you got into the car, Nalini taking shotgun with a deep shuddering breath as she lowered herself to her seat far more elegantly than your cap mobile deserved.

She was nervous, how cute.

"Hey, you mind giving me head while I get to my next stop?" You casually requested, before she could put a seat belt on.

"Not at all, sir." She was back to her customer service smile, it seemed to suggest she did mind.

Your mind almost immediately drifted back to the idea of going to the gym, seeing your older sister in her skimpy gym clothes and getting sweaty with her.

You tried you best to keep your eyes on the road after pulling out of the parking lot, even as you felt slender fingers picking at your zipper and trying to maneuver your iron rod out of your pants.

You didn't know how to feel about your sister though. Even now as Nalini slowly took your shaft into her mouth and fulfilled one of your teenaged fantasies of getting blown while driving, you couldn't shake the thought that if you were trapped in a gym with your sister you might not be able to control yourself. On the drive to the bank you had started to become incredibly horny incredible quickly. The same when you were standing over Nalini after emptying yourself into her mouth. A couple other events came to mind as well, a common theme among all of them was that it had taken every ounce of your willpower to avoid ripping the clothes of whoever you were leering at long enough to test the waters. You weren't sure you'd want to control yourself.

As you pulled up to red light, Nalini's soft lips rolling up and down your cock with a soft wet slurping you were somewhat chilled at what the wallet was turning you into. You were becoming sex addicted, you'd even go as far as to say you were growing dependent. Hell, you had what you could only describe as withdrawal, a couple times now, only instead of pounding headaches it was like somebody started smashing your dick with a hammer

A quiet chirping brought you out of your thoughts.

"Oh! Shoot!" Nalini let you out of her mouth with a soft pop then looked back at her purse beside her feet and worriedly up at you.

"Don't mind me, I'm the one who's not allowed to talk while driving."

"Oh, thank you!" Nalini beamed at you then gave your cock a quick peck.

Perhaps instead of your cheek?

Then she fished a phone out of her purse. "Oh! Hey baby!" Nalini gasped into the phone with a smile as she leaned back down towards your cock.

She took to absentmindedly stroking it with her free hand while keeping up a conversation,

"I'm just with a client... Oh no no no! He gave me the go ahead... I'm sure he doesn't mind...."

Out of the corner of your eye you could see her give you a rueful smirk before gently sucking on the tip of your dick.

"...Because he wouldn't have been the one to suggest I take my call if he did!" Nalini popped you out of her mouth to argue back into the other end of the call with exasperation but immediately took you back into her mouth as she awaited a reply.

You couldn't help but smile at how dutiful she was at her job. Or at the obvious affection she had for her fiancé even as she playfully argued. It was cute. Also she was sucking your dick, that was pretty great too.

As you thought about it though, it was great, but it was just that. It wasn't like the mind blowing body melting sensation like when you had to bone Christina or when you fucked Kari. Now that you think of it, both those situations were when you were suffering from withdrawal and were in genuine pain, not just afraid of it starting. Sure you had some pretty mind blowing orgasms the other times you'd taken advantage of women, but those other two times stood out as the only two that were paired with pain and they were pretty far apart, not only that, but there was plenty of build up. Maybe that meant that even if you got incredibly horny incredibly easily, to amounts that you had difficulty controlling yourself, you wouldn't be in agony so easily?

It was a pleasant theory, you could mentally restrain yourself but you couldn't will pain away. You somehow doubted you had the power to avoid jumping Caitlin's bones during a training session at the moment however. Though, you weren't sure how much you'd hate that anymore. You weren't sure if it was the wallet affecting you or it was just that fucking a couple girls in front of family uncovered just how deviant you really were. You weren't sure how much you liked or even disliked the idea either. You just knew that you shouldn't like it.

At that thought your mind drifted to your younger sister Dana, as you recalled her most recent employment was at a fast food restaurant. How would she react if you paid her a visit and gave her a hard time? She wasn't very cool headed, but she was probably desperate to finally be able to keep down a job at the same time. What about your mother for that matter? She was unemployed, living off survivor benefits, your late father's pension, and general frugality, but she did plenty of charity work and every so often took up odd jobs to make ends meet on particularly stressful months. And she always made sure to keep you up to date on when and where she'd be going. She was a prude by the standards you and your sister's set, but she was diligent in her work. If you tracked her down next time she took a job, how would she react…?

No! That's too far she was your mother! Your sister's were different… because… uh… because….

"Mr Thornton!" Nalini's curious shout drew the thought short.

"Huh! Yeah?" You were a little startled, some how managing to navigate a good chunk of your desired route on autopilot.

"I was just asking if you knew how long you were going to be keeping me?" She casually asked, phone still to her ear as she absentmindedly stroked your spit soaked meat.

"I-I'm not sure." Her description keeping her was exhilarating to say the least.

Maybe you should test some more boundaries?

"I was thinking the rest of the day… maybe more?" You hesitated to add the last bit, would that even work?

"Did you hear that? Oh, well, he said today at least, maybe tomorrow?" Nalini casually relayed your words, looking up at you for confirmation as she gently stroked you.

You gave her a noncommittal dip of your head, your cock twitching furiously at just what this meant.

"Well, just call me on my cell phone like you're doing now! I have it with me now and it's not going anywhere... Look, I can give you an update sometime when we iron out the time a bit!" Sounding exasperated Nalini groaned into her phone, stopping her stroking for a moment to shake her head. After a couple seconds she restarted her gentle ministrations and gave a gentle smile, "I love you too baby, kiss kiss." Then hung up and left the phone in a cup holder, "I swear, that man would be a mess without me." With a self satisfied smirk she took you back into her mouth.

"You must really love him." You commented, more to take your mind of your looming orgasm than anything.

You were pretty sure if you busted a nut in her mouth at the moment you'd probably run straight off the road.

"You have no idea." Popping your cock out of her

mouth Nalini beamed at you, giving a few happy tugs before going back to work with increased vigor.

"How'd he take the news that I'd be keeping you for a while?"

"Umm…." Seeing that conversation was now on the menu, she stopped sucking but made sure to give you a long slow lick from base to tip as she gathered her thoughts, "He didn't really mind. I mean he's six hours away so it's not long we had plans anyways, though." She sounded slightly confused, like she didn't know what answer you were expecting, like you were absurd for even asking that he'd have an opinion, "Oh, but when we got together he knew my job had me bouncing around a lot." She smiled up at you perhaps searching to see if one of her answers scratched whatever itch you were looking for.

You couldn't help but grin at the double entendre. Nalini didn't seem to catch it though, instead taking your smile as confirmation she gave you what you were looking for, she slipped the head of your cock into her mouth danced her tongue around your rod.

"So where are you staying? If you don't mind me asking since it sounds like you don't live around here."

You were almost there.

Both in her mouth and on the road.

"Oh, just some hotel." She gave a noncommittal answer.

What? Was she scared of you tracking her down and sticking your dick in her mouth?

"For how long?" You tried your best to hold off on your orgasm as you pulled into a parking lot and searched for a spot.

"Well I was told at least two weeks, but I was also told to be prepared to stay for a whole month."

"Must be expensive." You were just waiting for some mini van to pull out of a spot and you could unload in this busty bank manager without causing an accident.

"Well, I was given a company card loaded with what their accountant figured I'd need for a month, so I just have to be careful so I don't have to use my own money."

"Well then I've got a nice idea." You smiled mischievously, cupping the back of Nalini's head as she gently bobbed her head on the tip of your shaft.

She didn't release you, but tried her best to look at you curiously.

"You can forget the hotel and just stay with me."

"Umm I'm not sure if that would be appropriate…" She stopped all bobbing and started to sit up, "I did just tell you that I'm enga--"

With a firm hand you stopped her from rising and plunged her mouth back onto your meat, diving into the back of her throat and causing her to choke loudly.

"I don't think you get it!" You growled, hammering into her throat, to a symphony of gags and coughs.

Nalini rested her slender hands across your thigh, and it lead to a couple half hearted attempts at resistance, a light pressure, or bunching up some of your flesh between her fingers. Each attempt at resistance fizzled almost immediately though, despite the abuse you were giving her throat she remembered at the last minute that she had a job to do, and she seemed determined to see it through as best she could.

"You charged me forty fucking dollars for two pieces of

plastic just so I could use my money!" You howled and buried yourself into Nalini's throat, "Remember!" You screamed at her, but the only response was a messy cough sending spit across your balls.

You kept her pressed tight, her nose squashed against your pelvis as you started to bubble over, her throat struggling to eject it's invader pushing you the last bit over the edge. Then you started to blast load after load of cream directly down her throat. You had as much volume as ever and Nalini was starting to panic at being held down so long. Eventually professionalism and eagerness to please went out the window and she pinched and twisted at your thigh in protest for air. You hardly noticed however, you orgasm had taken over your mind. Keeping her down until the last load had launched down her throat was the only thing you could think of.

As soon as you stopped cumming your will to hold her down was gone. Nalini didn't hesitate to capitalize and sprung backwards, gasping for air. Several loads didn't make it down her throat and instead started to dribble down her chin.

You however, were feeling better than ever. You were starting to get used to the rush of orgasming now, just slightly. It was like drugs but better, you didn't feel the least bit impaired, just buzzed and full of energy.

Grinning down at the gasping Indian girl, her lipstick smeared, a mixture of saliva and cum coating her chin.

"I'm not offering you my place. I'm telling you that you don't need to worry about paying a hotel anymore because you're going to be working real hard to take the sting out of your outrageous fees. It's a lucky coincidence. I'm just being nice letting you know now."

"R-right." Nalini coughed and sputtered a bit, face still hovering over your cock, "M-my apologies sir. For the fee and my impolite assumption." Then with a shuddering gasp for air and a hesitant lean forward she gave your cock one last slurp, making sure nothing was left behind.

You could tell she knew it wasn't nearly as beneficial for her as you made it sound, but shining through the cum, spit, and fake smile was a genuine twinkle in her eye at what she was getting out of the arrangement.

You were completely blown away by her reaction. Or rather, what her reaction meant. You had just secured a busty house pet for the month and it only cost you forty bucks. All things considered getting robbed by your own bank didn't feel so bad.

You still needed to take care of your empty stomach though. For that matter, you'd be feeding two people now, wouldn't you? A practicality that you were now starting to consider with your head slightly clearer. You'd have to make sure you had enough cash.

Ah! Food-Whole! Your towns shitty excuse for a wholesale grocer. As far as stores in general went it was a depressing wreck. Concrete everything, ugly wilted produce, rotating stock, at least half of which was either damaged or nearing expiration. The best part being the shitty stock was all marked down to move them from the shelves quickly. The stores main clientele you were pretty sure were; restaurants who'd go through it as fast as they could buy it, and frugal individuals like yourself.

After all, even if the food was getting old or looking bad, as long as it wasn't actually bad it'd fit into anything that wasn't a salad just fine.

It definitely seemed the most cost effective choice. You were hungry and even if you hated what it would do to your wallet, passing up keeping Nalini as a cock sleeve in your dorm for an entire month was far too difficult for you to pass up if you could help it.

"You can stay here, I've got some thing's to pick up inside." You ordered Nalini.

"Yes sir." She was mostly recovered from the abuse you gave her throat, she sounded a little sore, but she had cleaned up the spit, cum, and smeared lipstick with some napkins you had lying around.

It probably suited her best to stay behind anyways. You had destroyed her undershirt and after a quick inspection you realized that she didn't leave her blouse top half unbuttoned on purpose, it was designed without half the buttons just to show off cleavage. You were reasonably sure she wouldn't have worn an undershirt if she wanted to do that.

Which seemed weird since she bought it…. Maybe she didn't have a choice, women's clothes were confusing.

With that taken care of, you slammed your junker's door shut, grabbed a shopping cart, and headed for the entrance. Grocery shopping always made your wallet quake, and the idea of shopping for two with your meagre savings made you want to puke, but the idea of what you'd get in return was pretty pleasing. Hell, maybe you couldn't keep another girl as a bedside cock sleeve for a whole month, but maybe you could have a wild night to take the edge off the beating your wallet was going to get tonight.

That brilliant idea in mind, you tried your best to make your rounds in the store as fast as possible while keeping an eye out for attractive workers.

No one in the produce section so you made it out with whatever looked the best while also not breaking the bank.

Some dude in the refrigerated section stocking milk.

Pass.

You got your cow juice and chicken babies and moved on.

Next was the deli. Deli meats were too rich for your blood, but they had massive logs of cheap mystery meat… you were pretty sure it was... mostly meat.... It tasted like meat and you hadn't noticed any strange mutations yet at least. Unless the mystery meat was the cause of the strange happenings to you and not your new wallet.

With a bit of a chuckle you pulled up to the deli, taking special notice of the workers behind the counter.

A dude, pass… too old, pass… Hello there!

Looking bored manning the counter was a petite looking girl. Maybe a tiny bit taller than your younger sister but just as slender. She had a short platinum-blonde pixie cut. It was a ruffled mess, but something about it almost looked intentional. Half of her hair was dyed teal in a fashion that made you consider that she had just let her hair grow out without touching up the dye, only you were bit skeptical that the pale blonde color was natural either. She had a cute face though, small and round with an adorable button nose. She had a heavy hand with her black eyeliner, but it really made her pale blue eyes pop, even from a distance.

Somewhere deep down you just knew she was the same age as your sister, all but confirming your plans for her, but you still felt it would've been safest to confirm things.

"Hey, there." You walked up to the counter and greeted the girl.

"Can I help you sir?" She sounded bored, not even an attempt at giving you a retail smile.

"How old are you?"

"Uh…." She started looking a little creeped out. "Eighteen, sir…." But apparently decided there was no harm in answering, "Do you need any meat sliced?" She was starting to look back towards her two co-workers.

"No, can't really afford it on my budget." You laughed.

"So is there something else you want?" She didn't really have the whole customer service thing down yet, did she?

You hadn't actually had your wallet long, but you were pretty sure you had a good handle on how to work it now and you could probably help her.

"Yeah, I do have some meat I think I need your help with." You grabbed at your pants with a dark grin.

"Dave!" The girl backed away and shouted.

With a sharp turn of his head, the man you spotted earlier stomped up. He was a great deal taller than you realized now that he was up close.

"Something the matter" He glanced between you and the girl.

"Um, this gentleman here needs some help." Her tone was genial, but her eyes screamed 'mental help.'

"I'm sorry, Emma's still new, she just started a few weeks ago. Is there something I can help you with?" Dave started to wave Emma off.

"No, actually!" You quickly barked. You were sweating, now, this Dave guy was a lot bigger than you, but you were pretty sure your wallet would work, "I was just looking to get my dick wet with Emma over there and she tried to pawn me off to you." You bit back a wince, just waiting for a fit to come your way.

Instead Dave sighed and turned on his heel,

"Emma, can you get back here."

The petite girl had barely made it a dozen steps away, and you saw her shoulders droop before she came back, looking pale and glancing between you and Dave.

"This gentlemen says you were refusing him service, is that right?"

"W-well no, I just, I didn't know what he wanted."

Dave cocked an eyebrow at you.

"I'll admit I might not've been clear when I said I had 'meat needs', So let me clarify." You locked eyes with Emma, "I want to stick my dick inside you."

She visibly flinched.

"That's not a service we offer!" She squealed, but she wasn't looking at you, she was looking at Dave, almost imploringly.

"You'll have to excuse her, this is her first job." Dave smiled at you, then looked sternly at the much smaller girl beside him, "Part of your job is helping customers where you can, do what he says."

Emma looked ready to protest, her face pale as she glanced frantically between the two of you, but after a moment she dropped her gaze to her feet and started to shuffle towards the deli exit.

"Wait!" Dave yelped, stopping the girl short. She looked back at him almost hopefully, and then, "Apron! Remember. Those aren't supposed to leave the meat department." With a gentle smile he held out a hand for the garment.

Emma looked crushed as she slowly undid her white apron, splattered with various splashes of red, then joined you on the other side of the counter.

With her apron off it was revealed she was dressed in a plain black short sleeved shirt, company logo emblazoned on the chest, paired with plain black work pants, both seemed a size too big for her. On her feet were matching black shoes.

"Move some groceries and hope in." You pointed into your cart with a smile.

You nearly had a heart attack when Dave stopped her, but you could smile at him now.

"You her manager?"

"Nah. I'm in charge of training her back here though."

"Oh, well could you tell her manager where she went? I don't think you'll be seeing her again today."

In your cart kneeling, Emma yelped and nearly dropped a head of lettuce she was moving out of her way, but Dave nodded with a smile.

"Oh! Should I get her things from the break room then?" Dave didn't seem fully sure if that's what he should've been asking, completely inexperienced with this particular happening.

"Uh… yeah, sure." After a moment's thought you figured it couldn't hurt.

A couple awkward minutes passed with Emma sitting in your cart, surrounded by various groceries, hugging her knees and refusing to look at you. A couple people walked by in that time, but no one seemed to pay you any mind, they just went down a nearby aisle while they talked about dinner plans.

Finally Dave returned, a simple, dirty, purple and at one point white, backpack in hand,

"This should be everything she came in with."

Emma snatched it from his hands and hugged it close, then went back to staring at the bottom of the cart.

With a quick thanks you tried to speed up the rest of your shopping, eager to play with your newest purchase.

The energy you got from your tumbles with Nalini served you well, people looked at you like you were crazy, but you were able to zip around the store without feeling an ounce of effort until you were almost done. After the fastest shopping you've ever done, you high tailed it to checkout. The whole way Emma didn't move. You almost felt sorry for what you were going to do to her. Almost.

While you unloaded your groceries, the old woman working the register gave the girl a quick hello before getting to work on your groceries, completely unfazed by that fact she was in your cart.

After squeaking back a greeting, Emma gave a long shuddering sigh then turned to you.

"So, how long is this going to take?" There wasn't a hint of her catatonic state up until now. Instead she had the air about her like she was asking whether or not it was raining outside.

There was no doubt in your mind she knew what you wanted, you made sure of that when you told her exactly what you wanted. It seemed she had finally come to terms with her predicament.

"Oh, I was thinking at least until tomorrow, but getting a good look at you it might be a week." You enjoyed being ambiguous, the idea was to see if she'd squirm, but there was a huge thrill that came with telling a girl she'd be locked in your room for an entire week taking your dick the whole time.

Emma didn't seem fazed anymore though, in fact the color was coming back to her face no longer sickly pale.

"Oh, okay. Where are you taking me?"

"Just to my dorm room, downtown." You were a little caught off guard by how little she seemed to care now barely even ten minutes later.

"I should probably let my parents know I'm not going to be home for a while then." She mumbled, mostly to herself and started rooting through her backpack.

With a bit of a smirk you loaded the last of your groceries and waited for your total.

"Hey mom! It's-- no I'm fine I just -- mom…! Mom…! No it's fine, I'm not going to get in trouble for calling you…! I think." Emma gave you a sidelong glance as she struggled to get a word in edgewise.

You just chuckled and shook your head. This was weird, kind of hot, but weird.

"Look -- No! I am working! A customer is just taking me home with him! He say's it's going to be--" She was cut off by a heart stopping shriek from the other end of her phone, forcing her to pull away from it with a wince.

You chuckled, until you were told your total. Luckily you weren't actually paying a cent for Emma, you could only imagine how much a petite high school senior would set you back, but you bought more food than usual with your new house guests in mind.

"Mom! It's fine! it's part of my job!" Emma shouted back into the phone, trying to talk over the hysterical shrieking from the other end.

You looked up at your cashier as she accepted your change, she was fighting back a chuckle while shaking her head.

"Look, put dad on the phone!" Emma eventually sighed as you started to wheel her and the rest of your haul towards the door, "Hi daddy...! No everything's fine, mom's just freaking out because I told her a customer is taking me home with him… yeah, Dave said customer service was a part of the job… yeah… I know, that's what I'm doing… between a day and a week, he's not quite sure yet, so I guess we'll see." Emma gave you a glance.

You couldn't help but laugh at just what was happening. You couldn't believe your luck when you found this wallet.

"I'll tell you as soon as I can when I get there… love you too daddy! And, when you manage to calm mom down, um, tell her I love her too." Emma then turned off her phone and tossed it back into her backpack, trying to use the bag to hide her red face, "Ugh! Parents!" She bemoaned.

In a way she reminded you of Dana. You wanted to say that turned you off, but you actually found yourself getting stiffer at the thought.

"I know what you mean." You chuckled, readjusting your pants.

Emma gave a nervous glance at your action, but smiled weakly at you nonetheless and lowered her bag.

When you made it back to your car you found Nalini had cleaned herself up nicely. She had her bra back on and you got a good look at it through her incredibly revealing business blouse. Most entertaining was how she was busy playing with her seat reclining function, looking bored out of her mind as she pushed it back and let it force her upright, rinse and repeat. For all her professionalism it was cute to see her do something so carefree. At least until she saw you and bolted upright.

"Wh-who's that?" Emma's eyes went wide and her voice was just above a whisper.

"Huh? Oh, don't mind her. I picked her up from my bank, she's just doing her job like you." You surprised yourself at how easy that was to say.

Emma didn't seem any comforted by that fact, she kept her eyes glued to the woman who was still too busy trying to pretend she was just fooling around with your car like a child to notice your new companion sitting in a shopping cart like a sack of potatoes.

For your part you were trying to load your groceries as fast as you could. Just like when you were a kid, you couldn't wait to tear apart the packaging on a new toy and play with it as soon as you could. Halfway through your haul a thought struck; you'd never had two women 'purchased' before. Even if that wasn't quite the right word it felt good to say, and it gave you an idea. Abandoning your packing for the moment you helped Emma out of the cart and opened the passenger door.

"Welcome back sir, who's this cute thing?" Nalini put on a real smile for the girl.

Emma went rigid, refusing to look Nalini in the eyes,

her cheeks going red.

"She's helping me with my shopping experience today, I'd like it if you could take her into the backseat and warm her up for me." You stroked the outline of your meat in your pants and grinned down at her.

"Oh, of course sir!" Nalini didn't hesitate to step out of the car and grab Emma by the hand.

Emma was just frozen, in shock or fear or something else you didn't know, but she seemed stupefied as the taller, older, and far more endowed woman gently led her over to the backseat of your car. She didn't so much as struggle when Nalini put some pressure on her to encourage her to lay onto her back. In fact Emma's only reaction came after her pants were pulled down to her knees and Nalini ran an appreciative hand over the petite girl's panty clad mound. Nalini started to pet the girl through her sky blue panties and in response Emma began to mewl like a kitten almost instantly and reached out to grab anything she could.

You kept watching as Nalini pulled the girl's panties down to her pants to reveal a wild, unkempt brown bush.

So blonde wasn't her natural color!

The busty Indian woman, follow your command, lifted the frozen teen's legs over her shoulders and threaded her head, through the gap and brought her lips down towards the girls fold.

You had to look away, with Nalini's skirt pulled tight over her pert ass, the quiet moans and gasps from Emma and just your power over them in general had you ready to jump them, but you decided it would be most practical to get your shopping out from the open and safely in your trunk. As you circled back to your cart and went back to work you heard a high pitched squeal behind you,

"Oh! Miss, are you okay?" Nalini immediately sounded concerned.

Emma's response was just a weak, shuddering,

"Uh-huh." But she sounded near tears.

You leaned around your open trunk lid to get a look through the back window and saw Emma, biting her lip eyes shut tight, her entire face going pink.

She sure liked being played with, especially for

someone that looked so heartbroken to be taken home when you first picked her up.

Nalini, from between Emma's legs couldn't see what you did though, so she seemed far less convinced,

"Are you sure? I didn't hurt you, did I?"

"K-keep going!" Emma squeaked as forcefully as she could, which wasn't very, her voice even cracked in the attempt.

God damn! You had to get your shopping put away, stat! You started throwing bag's in wherever you could and slammed the trunk shut just as Nalini commented,

"Oh my, you're drenched already!"

Oh man!

It was with a bit of hesitation you looked between your cart and the carousel a several dozen steps away, and the scene in your car. Nalini's giant bun gently bobbing up and down between Emma's slim, white thighs, Emma herself with a death grip on a seat belt and pushing against the driver's seat with all her might, eyes shut and panting.

You had better things to do, but still had some self respect. You weren't sub-human garbage that would just leave a shopping cart in a parking space to let someone else deal with. Even if you had two warm, wet pussy's waiting for you. You were still a decent person dammit!

It pained you to do it, almost literally, but you raced off with the cart faster than you could ever remember running before, then ran back even faster.

You were gasping for air before you made it even halfway back. Everything sex related aside, it was sounding like a better and better idea to take Caitlin up on her constant pushing to get you to train with her. Whether you were worried about doing her, or just dreaming about what you could do with a better physique, maybe you should be going to her just for your health and worry about everything else after....

You collapsed on your trunk with a heavy bang, determined to fuck the girls going at it in the backseat of your car, but your lungs protesting vehemently. If you had any surplus energy after running around the store, it wasn't enough for your fifty meter mad dash back and forth.

The sound of you hitting the trunk of your car and wheezing like a wounded animal drew a startled yelp from both girl's, however Emma quickly recovered,

"Keep going! I'm almost there!" She pleaded weakly, while reaching a shaky hand out towards Nalini.

"Th -- that's my -- my, job!" You drank in as much air as you could, while determinedly making your way around behind Nalini.

"Certainly sir." Nalini smiled over her shoulder and slowly began untangling herself from Emma's legs.

You stopped her with a firm hand on her rear, half for support, half to get a good squeeze in.

"Ooh!" Nalini squeaked at the pinch but came to an abrupt stop.

"While I... take care of... things here." You were starting to catch your breath and perk up a little, but you still had to take a moment to compose yourself.

You weren't sure if it was the squeeze or if it was just time, honestly both seemed plausible all thing's considered.

"I'll handle Emma, how about you get her to return the favor." With a deep breath you managed to finish your thought and straightened up to undo your pants.

You thought you could hear a disappointed moan from behind Nalini, but you couldn't tell through your panting.

"I think I can do that for you sir." Nalini backed up a little more as she gave her chipper reply.

Once she was free from between Emma's legs, she pushed them against the backrest and started to crawl over the girl, setting one foot on the floorboards and placing a hand on the headrest of one of the front seats. As she tried to maneuver herself forward she started to slip and put a forceful hand down just beside Emma's head, causing it to bounce in the seat. This time you definitely picked up a sound, this one a very satisfied groan, further supported by how she even started rubbing her legs together.

Emma seemed like a lesbian stereotype now that you looked at her, short, multi-colored hair… and… uh… she liked it when a busty twenty something older woman ate her out? That was lesbian, right? Her reactions seemed to suggest she had a thing for Nalini at the very least, but so did you honestly. Though she could just like the feeling of being dominated, you've met a few girls that had a thing for that.

"Don't hurt the poor girl." You teased Nalini, reaching in to give her ass a playful smack, "I still need her to look her best."

"Apologies sir."

"I-it's fine." Emma stammered, reaching a couple finger's between her legs.

"Hey! I said your orgasm was my treat!"

She didn't stop, either not hearing, or not caring.

You were honestly a little miffed, she was supposed to be following your orders.

Well, if you thought about it, maybe she didn't have to obey. From what you saw so far people could be as upset as they wanted, but it was your right to give her orders. Even if she wasn't magically compelled to follow.

Well, either way you'd say that was one point for liking it rough, she didn't sound like she was in the right head space to just be polite.

While you didn't want her to get herself off, Nalini was still in the way and that needed to be dealt with.

"Here!" You grunted and reached in, rolling up her skirt revealed burgundy panties pulled over her tight butt.

She caught on quick and pushed her hips backwards to give you a better position to slip your fingers under the thin fabric and work them down to her thighs. Then with a firm grip you latched onto her ankle on the leg pushed into the back rest and forcefully shoved it forward to work the panties off it without stretching them too bad. As soon as you let the garment go it snapped back to Nalini and pooled around her ankle. You didn't let go of her foot yet though.

Wrapping an arm around Emma's bunched up pants you yanked her backwards from underneath Nalini. She instantly began to crush her fingers with her thighs and let out a squeak and a moan. You kept pulling her until her hips were hanging out the edge of the backseat and her face was directly under Nalini's pussy.

That was two points for rough treatment.

"Thanks." Nalini flashed you a genuine smile.

Whether or not she wanted to be having sex with you or this girl, she seemed to genuinely like it when you made things easier for her and helped her out.

Then without any further words she spun around and sat down on Emma's face without any ceremony, crushing the girls head into the seat. Emma didn't seem to mind though, she yelped, but it turned into a hungry moan then you saw a tongue flick out of her mouth. She even drew back her hand from between her legs and put one hand on each of Nalini's thighs and seemed to be trying to pull her down onto her face even harder.

You were pretty sure that was three for liking it rough and at least one for liking pussy. It still wasn't entirely clear to you, but you definitely liked the idea that you'd be few dicks this girl would willing like take in her life.

With that thought in mind you hugged her legs together and pushed them over one of your shoulders and rubbed against her positively drenched slit. She tensed almost immediately, and Nalini's sigh told you the girl had stopped working.

"Don't be mean! After everything I did for you?" Nalini pouted, sounding heartbroken, but you saw a sly glint in her eye that said it was as much for your sake as her own.

You immediately felt a shiver go through Emma's entire body, half a second later, Nalini arched her back and sucked in a sharp breath while you sunk into Emma's warm depths. Instantly your car sounded like somebody was mixing a massive bowl of spaghetti. Emma was sucking and slurping at Nalini's juices and you started to hammer the girl without abandon.

It only took about a dozen thrusts before Emma locked up again and her pussy clamped down on you. Nalini noticed something too, she groaned, and started to grind against Emma's face. The girl seemed spent, her legs going limp in your arms as you pumped your hips against her's, but every now and then you caught a flash of her tongue stroking Nalini's fold.

"Give those here!" Nalini panted aggressively suddenly inches from your face.

A moment later she pulled back Emma's legs for you, unceremoniously pulled her pants and underwear over her shoes and hooked a leg under each arm. A moment later her soft plump lips were locked with yours, her hips grinding slowly against Emma's face.

"I'm almost there!" She pulled back and groaned, her warm, moist breath enveloping your face, "You want to be the one to do it." She didn't so much ask, as comment, pulling her crotch from Emma's mouth, the petite girl's tongue waving lamely at air not prepared for the disappearance of her little snack, a bridge of saliva connecting her to Nalini just a moment longer. She let out a disappointed sigh as her eye's fluttered open as if she had been having a pleasant dream.

You only vaguely understood what Nalini was getting at, at first. Until you realized you did kind of make it sound like you wanted to be the only one to make them cum. That's not exactly what you meant, but you weren't going to argue if that's how she interpreted it.

Nalini twisted in her seat, managing to keep Emma's feet push up in front of her as she did so eventually settling her pussy down just inches above the other girls. She looked back at you with a smile as your hips slapped against Emma's.

Grabbing a handful of brown butt in each hand you gave her pert ass a firm squeeze then swapped

Emma's pussy out for Nalini's.

"Ooh." Nalini arched her back and growled in appreciation.

You slammed your hips against hers and gave her heart shaped ass a quick slap enjoying it's short jiggle.

Nalini didn't respond to the strike, she merely bent down and slipped Emma some tongue, tasting her own juices on the girl's lips.

Emma seemed to be expecting, or at least hoping for it, melting instantly, shutting her eyes and kissing back full force, bringing a hand up and placing it at the back of Nalini's head.

"Don't stop." Nalini moaned, pulling away from the girl just enough to make out the words, "Don't stop." She repeated herself almost immediately after quickly licking the inside of Emma's mouth, "Please don't stop!" She chanted once more in a breathy purr

, inches from Emma's face.

You realized she was talking to you.

Well she did say please.

You kept a confident, steady pace, kneading her smooth rear end with appreciative fingers as she and Emma smacked their lips and sucked on each other's tongues. And then, Nalini drew back and purred a long low noise of ecstasy, her pussy shivering around you before she dropped her face down into the side of Emma's neck.

"Thank you, sir." It was barely audible over your hips, but it was appreciated nonetheless.

Emma was really getting into things now, capitalizing on the now vulnerable girl on top of her, leaning into Nalini's neck and started to kiss and suck her neck.

You could feel Nalini shiver again even as you slowly withdrew from her and swapped back to Emma. This time Emma didn't tense of freeze when you plunged into her, in fact she was gyrating her hips up and down as best she could while still focused on Nalini's slender neck.

You kept up the pace, hammering into one girl and then the other in succession until you were ready to burst.

"Come here! Let me cream your faces!" You didn't even let your order sink in before grabbing Nalini by one of her stocking clad ankles and dragged her backwards.

As soon as her knees touched pavement she spun around and leaned back against the car seat. Emma did her best to turn on the seat and push her head out beside Nalini. They both pressed their cheeks together and looked up at you with a breathless smile. Nalini's looked a little less fake than her usual. Emma's look was a little apprehensive, yet at the same time she barely even seemed to see you, off in her own world.

After several pumps you let out an animal roar and started to blast rope after rope of cum across both their faces. The first rope got them both, stretching from Nalini's cheek to Emma's. They both flinched, but where Emma kept her eyes shut, Nalini kept her's open, even going as far as opening her mouth and sticking out her tongue. Both targets were too good to pass up. You plastered Emma's face with cum, gluing one of her eye's shut, and painting several streaks across her forehead. Meanwhile you aimed for Nalini's mouth, but not very well, lining her cheeks with your over shots. When your orgasm finally subsided you shifted over and squeezed the last little bit out over Emma's tightly shut mouth, slapping her in the face a couple times with your depleted meat before tucking yourself away.

With a smile you ordered the girls to get ready to go and jogged over to the driver's side door. You weren't quite feeling in top shape again, but you felt remarkably good all thing's considered. That being said, looking into the rearview mirror and seeing Nalini help clean Emma off with her tongue you were pretty sure you were going to be feeling better than ever before you had to get back to the grind tomorrow.

While you were thinking up your next course of action you happened to glance behind you to see Nalini licking Emma's face clean like a hungry puppy, shooting you a wink and a cum covered grin.

Aaaaand… you were rock hard again.

This girl knew what you liked and was determined to give it to you. Now that was service!

Only problem being that you couldn't reasonably spend all your time fucking. Not like she wasn't giving you a heck of a lot of choice though.

Apparently there were downside's to having a magic sex granting object, like an insatiable lust that guided your every action. Who'd a thunk it?

After all, it wasn't like you could just abandon her now in an effort to save your productivity though. You already said she could stay for a month! You already bought enough food for her! You really really really wanted her camped out in your bed!

Fuck it! You had one more day off, so at least for today you could spend all your time fucking. For a few more bills you could have the best night of your life and maybe try and figure out more of what your wallets magic meant for you.

At some point in your deliberations the girls had gotten dressed, mostly clean and had come to the decision that Nalini should join you in the front seat again while Emma took the back. Both looked worse for wear. Their clothes and hair were disheveled messes, and their makeup was smeared. Nalini did her best to clean up her lipstick, but Emma had done her best to get rid of her eyeliner completely.

As you started to pull out of the parking lot with a destination in mind you made a quick order,

"Alright, we're going to be on the road for a bit so I'm going to have to ask for no more sexy distractions until we stop."

"I might be able to manage that sir." Nalini had a tone that suggested that it wasn't going to happen.

You were positive -- er, you were pretty sure, that she was just doing that for affect. Nalini was hard to read.

"Fine by me." Emma mumbled from the back, seeming like teenager that was forced on a trip by her parents she really didn't want to go on.

Now that you thought about it that wasn't too far off.

With a smile you pulled out of the parking lot. Your two passengers seemed unfazed by where their jobs were taking them. Emma, still pink in the face was looking out the window, trying to look bored, but her constant glances towards the front kind of ruined that. Nalini however looked actually bored, despite trying hard not too. She went between staring out the window silently to awkwardly giving you her fake smile, every now and then, seemingly unsure how to behave without being given an order.

God, 'give her an order!' Just thinking that had you hard! But you were driving, worst of all traffic was starting to pick up, if you got too distracted by getting your dick sucked you could get in trouble.

You needed to distract yourself or you weren't going to be able to drive in a straight line much longer.

"So, Emma, how's school?" You grasped the first coherent, non-sex related thought you could.

"Fine…." Emma gave a disinterested, non-committal answer.

"Oh! What year are you in? Do you like it?" Nalini

seemed to be eager to break the silence.

"Oh...umm, my final year, it's okay... math is kind of fun but science is a bitch. Our teacher sucks." Emma seemed far more interested in talking now.

Any other person and you'd just assume more involved questions allowed for more involved answers. But you couldn't shake a suspicion based on how much she seemed to like being between Nalini's legs... No!You were explicitly trying to avoid getting yourself horny!

"Oh, is it Mr. Gundry?" You tried to force your mind in a different direction.

"How did you know that?" Emma sounded both surprised and suspicious.

"My sister has the exact same complaints, I figured you probably have had classes with her."

"Who's your sister?" Emma sounded much more interested and much less on guard at the mention of 'sister.'

"Dana. Bendy girl, 'bout your size, in charge of the school's gymnastics teams. Won't shut up about it."

"Oh... yeah?" Emma was completely disarmed by your description, "I...I think I've seen her around before...."

Yeah, you bet. Seemed like maybe she was more disarmed by the idea that she now knew someone who was close to Dana.

"I got another sister too. Much taller, older, real health freak. She basically lives at the gym. She's a personal trainer and spends most of her off time working out."

From your side Nalini let out an interested hum,

"Oh that sounds interesting! I've actually been putting off getting into shape for ages. Maybe you could talk her into giving me a discount."

"Easily."

You weren't just trying to be nice, you could guarantee your sister would love to give anyone you referred to her a good deal, it was you yourself you doubted she'd go easy on. Especially if you sent her hot girls, it'd be her 'tax for helping you out.'

"How about you Emma, I'd bet you'd enjoy it." Referrals aside, you had ulterior motives for bringing Caitlin up.

"Maybe…." Emma did her best to sound uninterested.

From the rearview mirror you could see her eyes glued to the window, trying her best to appear passive.

"Oooh! Smooth, telling a girl she needs to work out!" Nalini chuckled and gave you a playful pat on the shoulder.

"Hey, I've got to help family when I can." You joked back, "Still, I'm pretty sure she'd actively try to make sure it was fun for you. Only problem is she refuses to wear anything that doesn't cling to her like shrink wrap. She also likes to get pretty grabby with clients once she's all sweaty if she thinks they're not working hard enough. Say's that 'if they're not willing to sweat it out properly she can at least share some of hers.'" The last half was complete bullshit, but you were trying to test a theory.

Nalini snorted and shook her head, smile on her face. Glancing in the rear view mirror though, Emma's jaw was hanging loose, working up and down soundlessly. You could practically see her drooling as the cogs worked in her head trying to compare this new mysterious sister to Dana in her head.

"I...I'll have to consider it...." Eventually she squeaked out, trying to sound bored once again, but failing miserably. She tried to cover the big stupid grin on her face with her hand, but you could still tell it was there.

That sunk it.

"Do you like girls Emma?" Nalini turned in her seat and smiled back at Emma.

Seriously? All your scheming and testing, and this one just out and asks?

"What!?" Emma's pink flush was gone now, her dopey grin while imagining your sister.

"Well, I'm just curious." Nalini quickly grew defensive, "You don't have to answer, I just get the sense you might enjoy the company of women more than men."

"Tell me about it." You rolled you eyes, in no small part due to her heavy handedness in the face of your calculated finesse, "She was eating you out like a starving animal but she didn't seem to want anything to do with my dick."

"I-I-I-I mean -- I didn't mean -- it's not like... I wasn't trying!" Emma looked to be having a panic attack in the makings.

"Whoa there, calm down girl! Breathe!" You were actually kind of concerned.

"Hey, hey, hey, calm down sweetheart." Nalini turned in her seat and in a gentle voice tried to talk Emma down from her hyperventilating, "None of us care who you're interested in."

You caught her giving you an evil side eye like a wife that just found out her husband told the kids Santa had developed a taste for children and was now on damage control.

"I'm sorry!" Emma was doing her best to control her breathing, "It's not that, not really… mostly…." She closed her eyes and started counting off numbers with her fingers before taking a deep breath and counting again.

Nalini didn't even hide her glare this time, it was like she was demanding you do something.

But what!? You weren't this girls fucking dad, you were barely older than she was!

"Look I didn't mean anything by it! I just meant it

seemed like you were having more fun with Nalini than me, I was a bit jealous, but that's it!"

You weren't sure if Emma even heard you, since she was doing breathing exercises but either way she seemed calmer.

"I've had some pretty bad issues with bullying, so it's kind of scary to be outed by strangers…" Emma sighed, finally in control of herself again.

You were willing to bet being trapped in a car with said strangers and having no clue where she was going probably made things worse.

"... but I mean, this is my first job... you aren't going to complain to my boss about this are you?"

In the rearview mirror you could see Emma giving you a pleading look with wet puppy dog eyes.

"About… you being gay?" How would that complaint even go over?

Nalini just stared at you with a blank look. It was kind of unnerving, how did things get so awkward!?

"About me breaking down, and not serving you

properly." Emma explained, looking down at her feet, "I've already messed up a few times at work and I've only been there a little over a week."

"Oh! That makes more sense!"

Everyone in the car except you visibly flinched, and you could swear Emma squeaked.

"Whoa! Hey! I'm not an asshole! Is that what you two really think of me so far!?" You took your eyes off the road just long enough to look around in a flurry.

"Not at all sir!" Came one hurried reply.

You couldn't help feeling Nalini was just putting on a customer service front though. She seemed to be able to turn it on like a light switch so it was hard to tell. Emma however seem genuinely defensive.

You decided not to answer. Normally you'd have been mildly hurt by such assumptions but shrug it off in a minute or two, but now you had the power to use it as an excuse to punish them... that was certainly an idea.

"...It's not that I don't like men... I just... prefer women...." Emma blurted out... for some reason.

It came out of nowhere, at least that's what you thought at first. It took a minute to understand she was answering Nalini's question from earlier.

"Well I suppose that makes sense…." Nalini murmured.

"Yeah, just because you like pussy instead of dick doesn't mean you hate men. Believe me, I know."

"No I mean, it's not that I don't like… um, dick." She was hesitant to say it.

You went to high school before, the swearing that went on in that place would make a sailor wrinkle their nose. She must've been considering her current position as a worker.

"I mean… I just never really think about it. It seems… weird. Like I know I'm supposed to like them, but they just seem like… I don't know, sausages and I not sure how I'm supposed to feel about them. But with girls I just know what I like about them."

So maybe she was a lesbian leaning bisexual than? Or at least wasn't sure if she was completely into girls. That even more ideas.

"Well then how about we work together? You tell me

what get's you going and I can try it out on you. That way you can get involved and actually serve me properly, and then we can brag to your boss about how good a job you've done."

"I guess." Emma gave a nervous chuckle.

"I mean, we're having sex right? So no reason you can't have fun too."

Now that you thought about it though, did they even see it as sex the same way you did? The wallet made them awfully casual about it after all….

"Yeah, I suppose. That would be nice." Emma giggled and sounded quite a bit calmer.

For the first time since you picked her up she didn't seem at all standoffish, or wary of you. She seemed to genuinely be warming up to you.

Nalini just smiled at you, like she was proud of you. Of how you convinced a troubled teen to agree to conduct raunchy sexual experiments with you. You were certainly proud of that.

But did this mean what you thought it meant? They legitimately saw what you did with them as sex, but there wasn't the usual taboo. Although, now that you thought about it, Christina didn't seem too pleased with having to blow you, even though that was long after you had the money to work your wallet. Oh! But she was full of smiles before you left… after you heard out her complaints about her life and complimented her a bunch.

You hadn't really had the time or even the attention span to just sit down and puzzling things out before, but the pieces were starting to fall into place. Sex with someone lost all taboo when you had the money and intent to pay for a service from them, but that didn't mean anything else changed. Just because you could bone them, didn't mean that had to like you, or even what you were doing to them, but since the sex was a complete non-issue you could still influence their opinions of you like a normal human being even while balls deep in them. Your mind was going wild with what this meant. You had so many ideas that even as your pants started to get painfully tight you were more than willing to hold off sex until you got some more ammunition.

"So, tell me a bit about what turns you on."

"Uh… okay." Emma took a deep breath before starting,

"I guess I like being tossed around a bit."

"Ah, you like it rough!" You nodded.

"Not exactly," Emma corrected you, "I like, uh, feeling dominated…? Like, I'm so much smaller than everyone," Emma let out a coy laugh, "so I mean, being treated like someone's toy just kind of feels… right? I guess…."

Your eyes shot up to the mirror. Emma was nervously rubbing her hands on her thighs, pink in the face. She seemed to be wincing at her own phrasing, but didn't looked like she thought it was necessary to correct herself.

"Ah, but you don't like being spanked or having your hair pulled then?" Nalini didn't seem the slightest bit nervous about the current line of questioning. In fact she had the air of talking about what everyone had to eat for breakfast.

"No!" Emma jumped and squeaked at the reminder that Nalini was in the car, "Sounds kinda weird honestly. Like I'm being treated like a child, or a whore."

"And you prefer being an object?" You couldn't hide your grin, not that you wanted too.

"In the bedroom." Emma nodded, with a deep breath, trying to calm herself down.

She was nervous sure, but her answers were coming so easy! This was amazing!

"What about you Nalini?" You gave a quick glance to the composed girl beside you.

"Me? Hmmm, well I suppose I don't have anything against being spanked or having my hair pulled. If it makes my partner happy then it's not that hard to do."

"That the kind of stuff you and your fiancé get up too?"

"Oh… no, not really." Nalini finally lost a bit of her composure, looking a little embarrassed.

How queer. She seemed so professional in all thing's sex, but the second her fiancé was brought up she got almost as nervous as Emma…. You'd have to consider exploring that later,

"Well what I meant to ask was what gets you hot and heavy than?"

"Right! Um, lets see…,"

Both you and Emma were at the edge of your seats waiting for her to grasp something,

"I guess I like gentler, more intimate stuff. I mean, I like having my body explored. Yeah, my girls up here are sensitive," To punctuate her words she pushed up her chest and wiggled in her seat a little.

Goddamnit woman! You had to struggle to keep yourself in control. You took a few deep breaths like Emma had and tried to calm yourself down.

"and, I mean look at them" Nalini added pushing up even more, "I can get why they take the main spotlight, but I like having the rest of me appreciated too."

Yeah not going to happen. If you looked down her shirt now you'd probably never get to where you were going.

"What… what's your favorite part of yourself?" Emma no longer seemed to be hiding her awe now that she was outed for having a thing for girls.

You were glad someone had something to say, you were still having trouble straightening your thoughts while keep straight on the road, and Emma's new open leering, borderline drooling, wasn't helping.

"You mean besides the obvious?" Nalini smirked.

Emma gulped and recoiled slightly, her eyes going wide. Nalini didn't wait for an answer though.

"It's hard to pick one. I like it when my feet are appreciated, especially when I'm getting a foot rub out of it. Working in heels all day is killer." Nalini chuckled, and had a distant look on her face, "Oh! but same for my back. I don't think there's a bra in existence that can take all the heat from these things."

"Ah, so you like massages then." You commented, finally regaining composure.

Breathing exercises really helped!

"What! No! Not just massages!" Nalini quickly became defensive… for some reason, "I…I uh, I like it when you played with my butt!" She seemed desperate to grasp something, unfortunately she didn't really pick the best choice, "Shoot. No I mean, like, I know my ass isn't much compared to my boobs, but walking around in heels everywhere isn't easy! So I liked that it's had some pay off. It wasn't that you rubbed it, I mean, I liked that, but I especially liked that you liked something other than my tits." Nalini finally seemed to find her stride and had regained her composure, and with a satisfied sigh added, "I like feeling like a complete woman and not just a vehicle for my boobies." She giggled, completely free of her nervousness from before.

"What about you Emma, you got a part of you that you like being played with?" Satisfied with Nalini's answer you tossed the ball back into Emma's court.

"Umm, my pussy? Heh..." Emma was still nervous though.

"Oooh! That's a good one too!" Nalini chuckled, "It's best if you focus on the clit!"

"Yeah, yeah I got it!" You rolled your eyes, "I'm not a total virgin."

"Uh!" Emma groaned loudly, and looked like she was searching for her words for a moment before continuing, "I am.... So... um, I'm not super sure about everything...."

"Really?" You were caught off guard by her revelation. She had seemed so adept when she was between Nalini's legs.

"Well, like, I've had some toys, and I, uh, sixty-nined a girlfriend once. But it turned out she just wanted to see if she liked girls and um… she didn't."

Nalini voiced her condolences at the hardships of finding love within the same sex. You for your part were worried they were going to try and change the subject and tried to steer things back to fetishes but were met with a lot of unsure answers.

"Okay, what about favorite sexual position, Nalini! Go!"

"Um, my fiancé and I usually do doggy style."

"And hide one of your best parts?" Considering what she said before though, you could see why she'd like it, "Whatever, Emma, go!"

"I'm not sure. Maybe the piledriver? It looks like it could be fun." She sounded like a girl trying to sound experienced.

Honestly you weren't even sure if she knew what a 'piledriver' was. You weren't even sure if you did.

"How do you girls feel about feet?"

Nalini's answer hadn't changed.

"I don't know. I guess maybe a massage could be nice." Emma seemed confused though.

"Skimpy outfits then?"

"Love 'em." Both seemed unhesitating to answer.

"Oh, you both like showing off skin?" That was a surprise.

"Who doesn't?" Emma scoffed confidently, "If you look good, you want to show off, it's awesome."

"For me it depends where. I can't dress like a hooker all the time, but I agree." Nalini sighed happily.

Not exactly what you were hoping for. There was a promising start, but they ended up talking like it was just fashion.

"Don't either of you girls ever fantasize about anything? Nalini! You're going to be married soon, haven't you done anything fun?"

"Well I had a wild time in high school, but back then no one was interested in anything but my tits." Nalini sighed, "My fiancé likes anal though. It's… alright."

"Um, my parents decided to block all the porn they could once I started dating." Emma turned her face away.

"That doesn't mean you don't have turn-ons! Jesus, work with me here! If you want to service me give me something to work with so I can get you off!"

"That's not really necessary sir!" Nalini jumped in her seat, looking confused.

What the fuck did she think you were getting at when you started asking about their fetishes!

"Yes it is! I don't know how it is for women, but for men if we don't orgasm we haven't had the whole experience. And I wouldn't be a man if I was willing to half ass it for you!" You did your best to sound noble, but you had some sinister motives.

They causally accepted you could fuck them, but that didn't stop them from enjoying it or hating it based on how you performed. So what would happen if you did everything you could to make them a quivering pile of mush in your bedroom now that you had the libido of a grasshopper. Would they become slaves to your dick? Or at the very least really like you?

"That's incredibly kind of you." Nalini didn't seem sure how to answer, but she seemed incredibly happy now.

"Oh, um, thanks…" Emma giggled in the backseat, "Um, I don't know how much I'd like it since I'm not super experienced, but I guess… I like being treated like an object."

"You said that already."

"No, I mean… like… uh, I said I don't like being treated badly, but I think it'd be nice if you just used me for, uhmm, your pleasure." Emma paused to chuckle as she tried to sort out her thoughts, running a hand through her soft hair.

From the mirror you could see she had her eyes squeezed shut as she went about composing herself.

"Like, I don't want to be slapped around, but if you just used me because you could…." Emma trailed off and you heard the sound of fabric shuffling.

You had hoped she was masturbating, but she wasn't quite there. She was rubbing her legs together though, and her hand squeezed between her thighs.

"Don't mind me, I'd actually like it if you flicked your

bean while telling me what you want me to do to you."

"I thought you said no sexy distractions?" Emma caught herself at the last second and bit her lip as she played with the waistband of her pants.

"Hah, I guess I did, then I brought all this up... forget I mentioned that."

Emma didn't wait another second before shoving a hand down her pants and letting out a satisfied sigh.

You were somewhat surprised at your own self control in all honesty. You really wanted to bone them, to the point where you couldn't think of anything but sex, but you managed to restrain yourself. Admittedly, just because your plans for later were more important to you.

"Mhhmm, there's some charm to that." Nalini groaned in agreement.

You now noticed she had her own hand slipped under her skirt. Whether she was getting as horny as Emma or just thought it was good service to give you a show you weren't sure.

"I think I prefer being wanted more than being used

though." Nalini started to get a little short of breath, "I love how when you use my mouth you still want more." Nalini grunted and started to work her fingers faster while bringing a hand up to her breast, "I love going for a second round. More if I can." Rubbing her breast over her clothes didn't seem to be enough for her, she slipped her hand under her half buttoned shirt and seemed to melt in her seat, "I want to believe that when you're with me all you're thinking about is taking me and using me!" Nalini let out a groan and seemed out of thing's to say.

All well and good though, you weren't sure how you managed to last as long as you did without fucking either of them, even pre-wallet you weren't sure if you'd have been strong enough. Now that the two girls you had picked up were jilling off in your car in unison, panting and sighing as if they were competing, you were just glad you had made it to your stop.

It was a long and difficult drive, in no small part because of your company, who were both currently pleasuring themselves at your command, aided by a long chat about their turn-ons. Somehow you made it an entire hour long trip without pulling over and porking them.

When you first decided you were going to have a wild Sunday you had considered several options, almost all involved amassing a bevy of babes and having yourself an orgy. In the end you had decided on quality over quantity. And you couldn't think of any better quality than Kari. At least in your experience so far she seemed like she'd have a lot to add to your party, more than a handful of random girls would be likely to add. Your new theory on being able to fuck girls until they liked you just cemented your decision to try and hunt her down. Especially after your little tiff with her earlier.

First thing's first though. You had an angry monster in your pants itching for some fun.

You kicked your driver side door open and started undoing your pants as you made for the back. Emma barely paid you any mind as she worked her fingers in her pants furiously, her other hand reaching up under her shirt to play with her modest chest. You brought that all to a quick end by roughly grabbing her by the front of her shirt and pulling her down onto the seat in front of you with her head hanging out of the car.

She squeaked in surprise at the sudden shift from sitting to lying on her back, and started to withdraw her hand from her pants but you grabbed her by the wrist to stop her. She looked up at you in confusion. Then you tapped her on the nose with your rock hard shaft. A look of apprehensive understanding swept over her and she opened her mouth dutifully, if not a little haltingly.

"Keep working." You nodded towards her hand as you let her wrist go and readied your meat.

Emma looked up at you, her mouth still open, and nodded slowly before she started working her fingers again, significantly slower this time.

Deciding to take a shot at her suggestion that treating her like a toy would be fun you plunged into her throat without another word or an ounce of ceremony. A shiver went up your spine the second her warm hole engulfed you. Emma however didn't seem to be having nearly as pleasant a reaction, her eyes started to bug out of her head, she started to hack around your cock and her back arched at the surprising new intrusion into her throat.

You brought a hand up to her throat in an attempt to keep her from breaking free. It took the fight out of her long enough for you to start pumping your hips. Emma didn't stop gagging though. She withdrew a drenched hand from her pants and grasped the wrist of the hand you had on her throat. When her slimy fingers started to dig into you, you took it as your queue to slow down a little at let her catch her breath. That didn't mean you had any plans to stop, you were trying not to be cruel, but that didn't mean she wasn't your toy.

Even as you slowed your pumping you leaned into her, placing a little more pressure on her throat, bracing yourself against the frame of your car to avoid crushing her windpipe. Emma still sounded like wreck as you rubbed yourself off using her throat, but something seemed to change for her. She seemed in a hurry to get her hand back into her pants, while the hand under her shirt was working it's way in small circles pretty quickly.

You'd been aching to go for an entire hour now, and seeing just how much she liked how you were treating her was too much. You started picking up your pace again. This time Emma seemed ready for it, almost hoping for it. She retched and wheezed as best she could with your dick filling her throat, her body convulsing as instinct said she needed the intrusion gone, but her mind was focused on her hands under her clothes.

You had to increase the pressure you put on her neck to get her under control so you could actually make each thrust, but that just seemed to get her going even more, her tongue weakly pushed past your meat to give you more room.

You were starting to seriously consider trying to hold back on cumming a bit longer, just to see how much better you could make things for her, but a beat later it was too late. Both her arms seized up and she brought her knees towards her chest, locking her ankles together as she gurgled something around your cock between coughs. That was it, you buried yourself as deep as you could in her throat and started to let loose. Burst after burst of jizz, right into her stomach. You barely registered Emma's slender, wet fingers weakly pawing at your wrist as the post orgasm rush started to over take you. Whether she was sapped by her own orgasm or lack of air, or she just seemed weak now that you were bursting with energy, you weren't sure, but she brought you back to your senses enough to realize you had been squeezing her throat pretty badly.

You whipped your arm back like you'd been zapped, pulled out of her mouth and took your weight off of her. Your last couple loads dribbling out of you, over her lips and onto the ground, joined by a torrent of spit and cum that got stuck in her throat and were dislodged by the coughing fit she had devolved into.

After tucking yourself back into your pants you got Emma upright and gave her a few apologetic pats on her back,

"Got a little carried away I guess." You chuckled awkwardly.

Emma shook her head slightly as she hacked a couple more times out the side of the car, sending a bit more spit and possibly cum inches from your shoes.

"No, it's fine." She had regained enough composure to talk, but she still sounded weak and gravely, "I know what I said about spanking and stuff, but having you grab my throat was pretty great." She sounded like a smoker and when she started to giggle she started to

cough like a smoker, but she looked happy. "Just…
maybe not so rough next time." After the most recent fit
passed, she brought a tender hand to the red hand
print marking her throat and gave you a weak smile.

"Ooh, does this mean I'm next?" Nalini purred.

Leaning over Emma to give Nalini a reply you noticed
that your mirror had been moved.

"Enjoyed the show did you?"

"You have no idea, but I've been waiting for you to
finish up with her so you can get me off…." Nalini was
breathless and no longer sounded like she was just
putting on an act for the sake of good service, she
seemed desperate to get off for her own sake.

Probably one of the benefits of no longer feeling there
was anything particularly dirty about wanting to be
railed by a near complete stranger thanks to your
wallet. She was of course keeping herself from
orgasming in the name of good service, thanks to a
slight misunderstanding about you wanting to
monopolize everyone's orgasms while they were
serving you. At the time it seemed like a great idea, but
the more you thought about it, there could be a lot of

fun involved with sharing the fun… that being said, for now you had other business.

You withdrew from the back seat and closed up and made your way to the passenger side. You pulled open the door and were immediately met with one of Nalini's shapely legs swinging out seductively, burgundy panties around her ankle, and pussy on display.

That kind of invitation was difficult to ignore, but you had literally just got off, so you were barely able to manage. You instead leaned in and locked lips with her. Nalini sighed, you suspected in disappointment, but her eager tongue spoke differently. She brought one hand to the back of your head and started running it through your hair frantically, her other hand with two drenched fingers rested on your cheek.

You weren't looking to make out though, so you broke it off as quickly as you could, her plump red lips latched onto yours in a futile attempt to stop you.

Despite her attempts to keep you, she didn't look disappointed that you broke away, in fact, she was reaching for your fly with a hungry glint in her eye. You were quick to grab her wrist and stop her though.

"Ah, ah! Not right now." You gave her a teasing wink.

"Oh come on!" She whined, nothing like her usual, composed self, "I can see you're still hard, just give it to me!" She gestured to the outline of your erection, bring forth the image to your mind of a drug addict needing her fix.

'Still hard' wasn't technically right. You had been getting soft after you unloaded into Emma's throat but Nalini had made sure to put a stop to that. It took plenty of self control to stop yourself, although it was a pleasant thought to consider it as good practice to avoid turning into some kind of monster, but the truth was, it was mostly just so you could have even more fun later.

That being said, you remembered what Nalini had told you earlier about how she loved being desired so you decided to take the edge off your looming refusal. Your hand still on her wrist you brought it up to your face, then took her two fingers still drenched with her own juices and stuck them in your mouth. Nalini seemed to melt instantly, her entire body relaxed and she started to play with your tongue as you sucked her fingers clean.

After you were certain you had every last drop of her

fingers licked clean you pulled back and grinned at her,

"I'm not done with you, but you're going to have to wait."

Nalini had looked to be in a dreamlike state until you told her she wasn't going to get fucked this second. She now looked like you just told her that she'd lost her job, but she put on a brave face and nodded.

"That's a good girl." You chuckled and gave her a peck on the forehead before turning around and heading for the bar.

You had a bounce in your step as you took pleasure in your own self control. You'd really like to say that you had more willpower than you had initially given yourself credit, but the cold hard facts were; you were super fucking horny, and you only held yourself back because you had bigger plans for later, it was practicality, not self control. Still, it was something, and you were proud. There was no way you were just going to roll over and let a magic item control you without a fight, even if being controlled meant loads of sex. It was the principal! Oh… and also you'd probably be broke and starving.... but those were just minor details.

A moment later your self satisfaction was destroyed, as the world was a cruel place that was desperate to balance out your incredibly good fortune so far.

"Sorry buddy, twenty bucks before I can let you in." A man blocking the stairway down to the bar calmly explained.

He didn't look sorry, you noted bitterly.

"What's this about?" You didn't feel it was necessary to hide your scowl, even if he was quite a bit more built than you.

You'd already been extorted once, but this time it wasn't by a hot girl with giant knockers who'd suck your dick… well putting it like that maybe you weren't_ exactly _extorted… but… uh, put a different way… um….

"You're not from around here then?" The man looked a little surprised but didn't wait for a reply, "Every third Sunday we've got live music playing from six till eleven at night. We've got signs hung up all over town advertising it and the bulletin board in the bar itself. Gotta pay the live music somehow."

Okay, that actually made some decent sense, even if

you didn't see any bulletin board the last couple times you were in. Only one problem,

"It's not six though."

"Sorry buddy, but my shift starts at five to keep people from trying to skip out on the charge." Taking a pause to look at his silver watch, you suspect for show given the speed of the glance, "Also it's seven thirty buddy, first set's nearly finished."

You merely blinked a few times then shook your head.

"Man, the time really flies when you're having tons of crazy sex." You then pulled out your wallet with a sigh. It hurt, but you already decided you were going to spend money to give yourself an orgy, and at least twenty dollars was a reasonable amount for a reasonable service. One you planned to milk for everything you could.

"Haha! I hear that." The man happily took your money and shoved it into a bag strapped around his waist, then stepped aside for you to pass.

"Say, is Kari still here?"

"Last time I saw." The man gave you a knowing grin,

"Good luck getting her attention though, she's been going on and on about this first set for weeks."

That was simultaneously good and bad news. Although, you just paid for a service -- hopefully one that bar actually hired -- so you could probably just grab her and walk out if you needed to. 'Probably' being the operative word. That being said this was as much a visit for trying to mend bridges with her as it was to get your dick wet.

Before you could even open the door at the bottom of the stairs you could feel a deep bass reverberating in your chest. It was nothing to when you were actually inside though. Apparently the acoustics in a giant, lightly furnished concrete basement were amazing.

Unfortunately quite a few other people seemed to have known that already. You had thought the place was packed on your first visit, but it was a miniscule crowd compared to tonight's. Enough to make you think there were some fire safety violation going on. But worst of all, you couldn't see Kari. She was quite a sight, arm tattoo, copper hair, plus-sized curvy, not the fat person pretending to be hot plus sized, an actual woman with a few extra pounds. But she was shorter than a good ninety percent of the people in here.

Remembering what the doorman had said about Kari really liking this current band however made it easy to think of a place to start looking. Easy to think, not do. You had quite a few people to rub up against on your way, some -- to put it simply -- were kind of gross, but quite a few of the others more than made up for it. As you got closer to where most people were centered and where the music seemed to be coming from, the crowd got thicker and you ended up squeezing past more than a few attractive girls. Some were wearing skinny jeans, other's mini skirts, some even yoga pants. all, you were certain, could feel your erection poking them, with how close everyone was packed. To your good fortune though, not a single woman seemed to pay you a shred of mind, even as you ground your dick into them on your way past. You gave plenty of 'excuse me's' and 'sorry's' but it seemed that anyone this close to the band had just learned to expect people to be touching them, or were otherwise too drunk to care.

By the time you made it to the edge of the crowd and in front of the musicians playing some sort of hard rock, a specific genre you couldn't quite place, your dick was starting to hurt something fierce though so you didn't care to try and puzzle it out. Not from withdrawal, but from being bumped and grinded against damn near a hundred lightly covered asses on the way through.

"Thank you!" A conventionally attractive man boomed into a microphone, just a couple feet away, causing you to wince. He had a thick accent, you couldn't quite place over the noise, but it didn't seem to hinder his grasp of your language.

You moved to cover your ears at the high pitched shriek that the crowd returned to the thanks. It didn't take you even a second to figure out why. The man at the center of the crowd looked like a Swedish super model. Sharp jaw, elegant golden hair, sweaty, or more likely oily, abs on display underneath a sleek leather jacket, that explained why you found so many women in the crowd.

"That's it for us though! We could all probably use a drink, I know I can." The man chuckled at his own… joke? and was met with hoots and hollers from the inebriated women squeezed together, "Singing really takes it out of a guy!" More screams followed, "And we should let some of these other acts get a chance to play! Let them see just how great a crowd you are!" Yet more, senseless drunken screeching. At least you sort of got the reasoning that time.

He seemed like a nice enough guy to be honest, based on ten seconds of talking, but just seeing how handsome he was pissed you off. The rest of the men with instruments seemed to be lookers too. The drummer was dressed up like a moody punk, heavy makeup, messy hair and all, but he was smiling brightly, also showing off some pasty white abs, minus the glossy sheen. Some guy with a bass looked pretty similar to the singer, but with slightly more tamed hair and actually had enough clothes on to cover himself, you liked him the best.

Jealousy took root when you remembered Kari had been 'talking about them for weeks.' You weren't ugly, and you'd like to think that was objective, but you were pretty sure you didn't hold a candle to any of the guy's on stage. You were in complete different leagues. Them with their looks, you with.... your looks... plus a magic wallet. Practically speaking, you didn't need to be jealous of them, honestly you weren't even in competition, but you couldn't control your emotions, just how you reacted to them.

Even if Kari had a thing for one or more of these pretty boys, that wasn't going to stop your plan. You'd just have to try and tactfully take her away from them without making her hate you.

You quickly scanned the front of the crowd for any sign of Kari, hopefully the band finishing their set didn't give her a reason to immediately get back to work. Although… if it did, that would've meant she just liked their music.

Just then you spotted her, a drink in each hand, ear to ear grin plastered on her face.

"Hey! Kari!" You immediately started working your way over, but it was slow goings, wading through the crowd.

Kari looked around in shock for a minute before she spotted you. You could see her recoil slightly, before an amused smile replaced her giddy grin and she waved at you.

Just as you got within a dozen steps or so and started to shout again she turned and wrapped her arms around a tall, slender dirty blonde figure and was swept into a crushing hug. Kari doing most of the crushing, actually lifting the much taller person off the ground.

You did your best to not frown at the affections between them, it wasn't like you were actually competing with anyone, but you weren't able to hide it very well. You did at least try to assume a neutral expression as you made it the last little way.

"Oh my god! It's been forever!" Kari squealed in joy.

And then Kari released her bear hug and you saw… boobs. Not just Kari's boobs, but smaller perkier boobs, squeezed into a black corset. A pair of plump ruby red lips brushed within inches of each of Kari's cheeks as the tall blonde touched her own cheeks against Kari's. Your eye's instinctively flicked downwards to take in the entire figure, undoubtedly feminine now that you thought about it. You were drawn in by her firm ass and legs hugged by shiny black leather pants, down to her black ankle length high heel boots on her feet.

"Oh, hello?" The woman, now right in front of you gave you a pleasant smile and cocked her head to the side. She had just the barest hints of a Swedish accent that betrayed her origin.

She was just as beautiful as the rest of the musicians. She had a softer rounder face than the men, a sharp nose, and keen brown eyes, and a complexion only a couple shades darker than Kari.

You could hardly believe you missed her before. A

quick glance at the clear section of floor that was serving as a stage told you that the only instrument you hadn't noticed before was a keyboard, with microphone in front of it and chair behind it. That probably explained it.

"My, my, three visits in two days? I'm going to have to learn your name soon, won't I?" Kari popped open the bottles she had in each hand, presenting one to her friend giving you a smile and a chuckle.

"Ah, got yourself a new regular do you?" Kari's friend smiled and nodded.

"Haha! Well what can I say, this place is pretty dope. And now I know there's live music once a month, it's been growing on me. Although… I'd say Kari's the biggest part of it."

"Oh, look out! You've got another guy after you!" Kari's friend jabbed Kari with an elbow.

Kari shot her friend a withering sneer in response. It was the best she could manage after your compliment on her establishment seemed to cement her grin into place. Your compliment on her seemed significantly less effective, but her smile still grew by a hair.

"Well what can I say, her service is amazing."

"This one's?" The tall blonde gestured towards Kari, a smirk on her face.

"Oh shut it!" Kari slammed her bottle on top of her friend's causing the blonde's chilled beer to start foaming over almost immediately.

The blonde didn't even have time to snap back at Kari, she quickly shoved the neck of the bottle between her juicy lips, sucking down the drink as fast as she could, white foam dripping down her chin from the foam she that didn't make it into her mouth in time.

Before you knew it you were adding,

"Well she was a bit grumpy my first visit, but she sucks dick like a vacuum."

The blonde seemed to freeze for a second. Drink still tipped back, but her eyes were flicking between you and Kari rapidly. Kari was frowning at you. Then a moment later, the slender blonde lowered her drink with a satisfied gasp and inclined her head,

"Sound's like she hasn't changed since college."

"Really, you want to do this?" Kari scowled at her friend, but you could see her fighting a smile. Then she shook her head and turned back to you, "Astrid and me go way back. We're super close friends."

That's when it struck you that she had been expecting that retort and had been bracing for it the second you mentioned sucking dick.

"Oh, that's interesting. I'm Jason! Nice to meet you." You shook Astrid's non beer soaked hand then added, "How close are we talking?"

"Yeah, no. Get your head out of the gutter." Astrid rolled her eyes and put on a wry smirk.

"Well…." Kari mumbled into her drink, cutting herself short by tipping it back.

"College doesn't count!" Astrid snapped.

"If you say so…." It was Kari's turn to roll her eyes and smirk.

There wasn't any question anymore. You were taking them both home with you, no matter the cost, here and now.

"So how'd you like the show?" Astrid smiled at you and took another swig of her drink.

You didn't particularly see any reason to lie, so you merely apologized for your lateness while you drank her in and contemplated how you'd broach the subject of fucking them both.

"Ah, well that's too bad. We've got a CD by the door though, you should definitely check it out."

"It's great, she has a beautiful singing voice it really pairs great with Olof's." Kari put forth her attempt to hock her friends merchandise.

"That the half naked oily dude?" You took an educated guess that it was the only person with a microphone you saw up there and a chorus of chuckling from the girls was your answer, "Well maybe I'll take a look. Do you come with it?" You dove straight in and winked at Astrid.

She smiled a bit and snorted,

"I don't think buying a fifteen dollar CD is quite enough to woo me."

"So you're saying I have to buy something else too?"

You sounded disappointed, not an act, but you were pretty sure they didn't know that since they both smiled a little brighter at your 'joke.'

"I'm sure they'd love that!"

You were suddenly slapped on the back by a hard hand, a thick Swedish accent screeching through your ear. Less muppet chef, more Viking. It was Olof, the singer.

"Goddamnit, could you just butt out?" Astrid wasn't the slightest bit smiley anymore, she actually looked a little scared.

Yeah, you didn't like this Olof guy one bit.

"What's the matter? This is a paying customer right?" Olof however just had a big stupid grin on his face, looking around between the three of you like a curious puppy.

"The problem is, I don't think Astrid really wants to spend to whole night with a dick in her mouth." Kari placed a gentle hand on Astrid's shoulder, a warm smile on her face, "We really wanted to catch up."

"Actually I was thinking he was asking for a date, but

sure." Astrid bobbed her head from side to side before downing the last of her drink in one deep swig.

"Well it won't just be her mouth." You didn't hesitate for a second, emboldened by the casualness of everyone.

"Ah hah, yeah, but I'm not sure how much we'd be able to talk if we let you have at her." Kari let out a wistful sigh, an exhausted smile on her face as she winked at you, "And she's only in town until tomorrow night. Then there's the fact that I'm actually, technically still working right now so I'm technically supposed to serve customers... but I'm trying to spend as much time with Astrid as I can." Her eyes met yours and she seemed to say, you should just drop the issue.

"Actually, that's perfect!" You weren't going to relent though, after wading through a sea of barely dressed asses and rubbing up against nearly everyone you weren't going to leave without some more pussy, "I wanted you to join us."

Kari's face immediately fell and she looked kind of disgusted.

"Look, I know what I promised you this morning, but can you blame me? After riding you once it's kind of hard to quit cold turkey."

Kari's face drooped from hard disgust to crushed disappointment, somehow that hurt more.

"You got money this time?"

"Uh, yeah." You gave a nervous chuckle.

Some apology this was turning out to be.

"Two shots of your strongest stuff please." You paired with a wink, remembering the other part of your promise.

This time Kari started to smile weakly, but it seemed clear that she wasn't particularly happy.

"Oh, uh, for both of you though, I've still gotta drive you two back home with me." You still wanted to apologize, but you weren't going to back down from getting them on your dick

"Look, I'll suck your dick, or whatever, but I'm staying to talk with my friend." Kari didn't look to be backing down anytime soon.

"I suppose I could help out too if you're going to be

buying a CD but I'm with Kari." Astrid looked like she just bit a lemon in half.

"No, this is perfect!" Olof bounced on the balls of his feet like a child, "You both get a drink on him to celebrate, then you can go home with him--!"

"No! Nope, no! I'm a grown ass woman and I've made up my mind!" Astrid stood up to her full, impressive height, and stared Olof down, she didn't look scared in the slightest now.

Neither did Olof for that matter, he still looked like an excited puppy,

"--Where it's nice and quiet." He had waited for Astrid's interruption before jumping straight back into his explanation.

Immediately Kari and Astrid's faces were expressionless as they considered this new bit of information.

"I mean, if you're both half as wild as Astrid's told us two of you and one mortal man shouldn't take up too much of your time."

Kari and Astrid exchanged a glance and a smile started

to creep onto both their faces.

This Olof guy wasn't half bad.

"The keyword there being mortal. But I can just tell Cliff I'm serving a customer." Kari's smile grew bigger and bigger until it peaked at her demanding drink money from you.

You forked over a painful amount of cash for a couple shots, but looking over what you'd be getting in return as they sauntered off helped soothe the wound.

"Grab your CD and we'll meet you at the door." Astrid gave you a seductive wink back at you before following Kari through the throng of people.

"Hey!" Olof shouted in your ear and forcefully spun you around.

His handsome face was just inches from yours, his pearly white teeth bared.

"Thanks for this, friend. Astrid was going to kill us if we didn't make a stop in this town. We just barely squeezed it in." Olof's laugh didn't suit him. He absolutely sounded like he had just crushed a village in a brutal raid. "Oh, and don't tell Astrid I did this, but I'll set you up with a free poster, one of our juicy one's, yes?" He whispered into your ear, it just didn't feel right without a hairy beard to scratch you with though.

Still, this Olof guy wasn't half bad!

"Lead the way!"

You both slapped each other on the back in a forceful, violent show of camaraderie and started to push and shove your way to the door. Luckily Olof took the lead like a linebacker, knocking people left and right. Most of them were women, and most were considerably less upset once he flashed them a mildly apologetic grin then you came in and muttered a proper apology to really drive things home. You both made an excellent team.

With Olof plowing through the crowd you managed to make it to the other side in a fraction of the time it had taken you to make it through the first time.

"So what songs did you like?" Olof turned to look at you once you made it to the merch table.

You told him the truth and he seemed genuinely sorry for you before he swiped a case off the table,

"You should probably just take this then."

Shoved into your hands was a CD in an old fashioned jewel case. On the front was a nice picture of a some tropical beach; white sand, crystal blue water, you saw some palm trees in the distance, some massive moss coated stones dotting water's edge, and smack dab in the middle dominating the foreground was Astrid's firm rear end, a soaking black bikini sticking to her skin. Her ass was being pushed back towards the camera as she balanced a multi colored beach ball on her hip. She was looking back over her shoulder and down towards the ass-level camera, comically large sunglasses pulled down, a tired smirk on her face. Off to one side of her, a short ways into the background was Olof and the bassist in swimming trunks, building a sand castle and on Astrid's other side was the pasty skinned drummer pretending to get a tan. All three men were currently distracted by a giant serpentine dragon bursting from the water behind the giant rocks in the background and dwarfing them.

You were immediately reminded of Kari's sleeve tattoo.

All thing's considered, it was an incredibly high quality image for a CD cover of a band you've never heard of before. It was twenty-two bucks though, a little more than you were expecting.

"Astrid's the lead singer in most of the songs and it's even got five bonus tracks." Olof shook you by the shoulder excitedly.

"You think this'll earn me brownie points with her?"

"If you play it off right maybe." Olof for once didn't sound excited, well, as excited.

He was currently rooting through a pile of cardboard tubes. It didn't take even a minute before he found what he was looking for though, and once he did his eye's lit up once more and he shove the tube into your chest, grinning like a kid on Christmas.

"This will help though."

You popped plastic cork off the tube and slipped out a roll of glossy paper from inside. You gave Olof a curious look but he just gestured for you to continue. It was a big poster, you couldn't unroll it in it's entirety at the moment but you could see enough.

A new Olof fanboy was born that day.

It was the same art as the CD cover, but over twenty

times the size, must've been at least four feet long and it was in HD. You could make out every single bead of water on Astrid's exposed flesh. You could see several errant wet hairs stuck to her cheek. Every wrinkle in her clothes, even the slight crease of her wet bikini bottoms finding a way to squeeze between her cheeks. If you didn't know better you'd have thought you'd be able to see yourself reflected in her hazel eyes.

You were speechless. You returned the poster to the tube and looked it over for a price.

Two-hundred-and-twenty!

You were horrified!

"Juicy poster, am I right?" Olof winked.

"...Free?" You struck dumb and struggling to make any kind of coherent noise.

Part of it was the straining in your pants of the image of Astrid's half naked, wet body on display, in it's highly defined glory, but a two hundred dollar gift from a guy you just met was it's own kind of mind blowing.

"We barely sell these anyways." Olof waved you off.

That hardly rationalized it for you though.

"Just try to make sure Astrid has a good time with her friend." Finally there was only the barest hint of Olof's boyish excitement, instead there was a much more sober smile, "We'd still be playing in Loffe's garage if it wasn't for her. I'm certain. It's weird, but this might actually mean more to us than it does her, but if you want to thank me...." Olof laughed and scratched his neck, his eyes turned towards his feet.

"You do not have to worry." You mustered more conviction than you'd ever had before. You were already scheming to see if you could manipulate girls into being happy.

Olof broke out into a massive grin and swept you into a hug.

"Okay, we're ready." Kari came up from behind you, pinching you on the rear as Olof held you hostage. She was slurring a little.

"What'cha get?" Astrid was slurring a lot, and giggling periodically as she looked you over.

You doubted the cash you forked over was enough to do that, but that didn't particularly matter as long as they were drunk somehow.

Before you could answer, Astrid swiped the tube from your hands and glanced at it. Instantly spotting what he wanted she started to chuckle,

"You have good taste."

"Lemme see." Kari swiped the tube from Astrid and turned it over a bit, "Jay-sus! You just got hosed!"

Astrid had been smiling at the case in your hand until she heard that, then she started to stare daggers at Kari.

A sharp elbow from Olof told you it would be best if you interrupted before their inebriated minds managed to piece together a college student that was flat broke several hours earlier probably couldn't pay for something like this.

"Well I don't know about that, but I'm afraid I'm not going to be able to give you a conventional tip this time. But I'll think of something." You winked at her, grabbing the poster back from her without resistance.

"Kari's told me about that." Astrid snorted, "I'd like to see for myself though."

That was the easiest promise you'd ever made in your life. In fact, with the poster still fresh in your mind you were seriously considering giving her a taste of things to come right now.

"Wait a sec!"

Kari gave you a curious glance over her shoulder, stopping with her hand on the door knob. Astrid turned on the spot to face you. Without any further explanation you started to take off your pants.

"Seriously...?" Astrid tapped her foot a couple times.

"Can't even wait till we get to your car?" Kari sighed, and sauntered the few steps from the door back to you.

"If I recall correctly I bought two drinks and that's your price to stare." You dropped your pants with a grin, revealing yourself at full mast.

Kari gave a tired laugh and shook her head,

"Yeah, yeah." She took a deep breath, then pulled her shirt over her head, and slung it over her shoulder. A moment later her bra got the same treatment, "This better?" she shook her impressive chest from side to side, an exaggerated pout on her face.

You took note of her frequent glances down to your exposed member. Astrid however, was full on staring as if she'd never seen a dick before. Awkwardly enough, Olof was still standing there too, and he gave your cock a confused glance, then he looked over to Astrid and Kari, and suddenly the handsome singer's face transformed from confused to one of dawning realization. With a pearly white smile he gave you an enthusiastic thumbs up.

It really drove home the fact that even if you were allowed to be nude now -- logically you assumed only while getting serviced -- it was honestly kind of uncomfortable. Perhaps you'd have to practice and get used to it. You were reminded of your last session in this bar where you were cheered on. Maybe you could take your fun to some other public places some time.

For now though you had to focus on what was in front of you,

"I love it." You gave Kari a warm smile then took a breast into each hand.

You gave each mound an appreciative squeeze, then started to play with them, lifting them from her chest and admiring the soft weight. You ran your hand around the outside of them, tracing her chest with your finger tips before scooping her tits back up and rubbing your thumbs over her nipples until they began to stand to attention. The whole time Kari didn't break eye contact, a mildly amused smile on her face. The only sign you were getting to her besides her hardening nipples was a slight flush appearing in her cheeks, but that might've been the alcohol.

"I think I could use a blowjob though."

"Seems so." Astrid let out a long sigh, but got to her knees all the same.

"You too." You fixed Kari with a hard stare and tweaked her nipples sharply.

Kari squeaked and bit her lip, jumping slightly before giving you a sultry wink and dropping to her knees beside her friend. Once they were both on their knees they leaned towards each other, your cock the only thing keeping their lips from touching. You could feel their warm, moist breath over every inch of your shaft. Their eyes met, and after a moment they shared a laugh at some unspoken revelation, then in complete sync they pressed their tongues against their respective side of your cock and gave you a long slow lick from base to tip. Once their tongues met at the end of your length they leaned forward and locked lips around the head of your cock.

It was difficult to tell whether Kari and Astrid were trying to make out with each other or were trying to kiss and suck the head of your cock, the only hint that it was the latter was their sparkling eyes looking up at you as they went to town on each other around your meat.

Your cock twitched at the mere sight of the two gorgeous girls submitting to your desires.

As if that twitch was some kind of flag drop, both girls separated and started getting into position with a confident, seemingly practiced, efficiency.

Kari straightened up and shuffled over to be directly in front of you then slowly and confidently skewered her throat with your meat, not breaking eye contact the entire time. Astrid at the same time crawled over to your side on her hands and knees and ran her tongue across the underside of your sack.

You nearly came right there. Your cock twitched powerfully even while lodged deep in Kari's throat. The movement caused Kari to gag slightly, her eyes started to bulge just for a second, and she drew back quickly.

"Liked that did you?" Kari gave you a mischievous grin of her own and licked the spit from her lips.

"Well, have fun friend." Olof suddenly reminded you he was there with a pat on the back, then leaned in and whispered, "If possible, try to have her back by tomorrow night please. We have a schedule."

"I'll... see what I can do...." You were shocked at the interruption, but most of all weren't sure you would be able to keep a promise like that so you tried not to actually make it, the sight between your legs was one you could definitely get used to.

Kari wrapped her slender fingers around your cock and bent you upwards, leaning her face under your balls and gave you a savoring lick of her own.

"Back off! This is my turf!" Astrid snapped with a smile, leaning in to give Kari a quick kiss on the lips, slipping in some conspicuous tongue.

Olof didn't have a response to your weak half promise, he merely patted you on the shoulder a couple more times and walked off without another word, dopey grin still on his face.

You felt a little bad even imagining jipping Olof after the help he gave you, but you were also pretty sure both girls would appreciate the extra time together as much as you would.

Kari, having been chased off by the territorial Astrid, went back to the length of your meat, sucking the end of your cock like a lollipop. One of her hands found it's way around behind you and clamped down on one of your butt cheeks with far more force that you were expecting, startling you deep into Kari's throat. Kari choked slightly at the roughness, but recovered quickly and gave a satisfied hum that sent a shiver up your spine. Kari's other hand, far more gently,found its place rubbing up and down your pelvis and beginning to explore under your shirt. Her slender, cool fingers felt surprisingly incredible against your stomach as half your focus was still on the entirety of your cock was being kept nice and warm by a pair of mouths.

You were taken out of the moment when the door just a couple feet away opened and a small party chatting away nearly walked right into you.

"Oh! My bad!" A girl in a denim jacket gave an apologetic smile down at Kari.

"No no, we're kind of in the way here!" Astrid, seeing Kari was a bit occupied, quickly waved things off between licks across your sack.

"Oh, hey Kari! Been a while." A plain looking man in the group gave Kari a tap on the shoulder, stopping her bobbing cold.

Kari gave you one last bob before pulling away and turning around, her brow furrowed in confusion. As soon as she saw who had tapped her though her eyes lit up,

"The fuck have you been all this time." Kari sneered and chuckled playfully punching the man in his shin.

"Oh busy as hell. Kinda like you are now I suppose." The man pointed to your crotch where Astrid was sucking on one of your nuts.

"Yeah, I bet." Kari rolled her eyes and gave you a gentle tug.

"Oh screw you!" The man shook his head, "Anyway, I should probably let you get back to work, maybe we can catch up when you're done here." The man gave Kair one last pat on the shoulder and gave you a congenial nod and a smile.

"I wouldn't count on it." Kari shrugged and took you back into her mouth, bobbing vigorously in an instant.

The man expressed mild disappointment, but quickly recovered as he raced off to catch up with his party.

"How about we get out of the way." You weren't particularly comfortable with where you were anymore.

Just because you could get blown in plain view of a crowded bar, didn't mean you could block the entrance, that was just indecent.

You didn't wait for the girls to respond, you just slowly started walking backwards. Kari didn't seem hear you though, or if she did, hadn't cared. As you took your first step backwards you pulled yourself free from her vacuum-like mouth with a loud wet slurp, getting a curious glance from a few people wandering around nearby.

Astrid seemed just as resistance to let you go, she did her best to follow without letting your balls out of her mouth, but it was difficult. You ended up easily out pacing the girls as you back pedaled to the side of the merchandise table, out of the way of most foot traffic. The girls crawled on their hands and knees after you, like a couple of hungry puppies.

"That's better isn't it?"

Neither girl responded with words. They did change up their tactics however. Kari took one side of your shaft and licked up your length with long strokes of her tongue, while Astrid took to kissing and sucking at the opposite side of your shaft.

That was as good a response as any. In fact you were nearing another orgasm and you let them know with an appreciative groan and a pat on each of their heads, treating them like obedient puppies.

Kari and Astrid froze for just an instant and locked eyes, immediately you could see a change come over them, there was no flirtatious glances up at you anymore, there was only a lusty hunger in their actions.

In perfect unison they both lowered down to your balls and gave you a quick lick up to your tip. There was a momentary make out session around your cock before Astrid took command of blowing you. A quick huff from Kari however convinced you that it hadn't been making out but a struggle over who got to suck you off.

Kari glared up at you and wrapped her slender fingers around your shaft, working half of it slowly while Astrid sucked on the other half frantically,

"Since she wants it so bad, how about you give this dirty slut her reward." Kari bared her teeth in a sneer and put a hand on the back of Astrid's head.

Not one to disappoint a request from a beautiful woman, especially one jerking you off, you let out an animal groan and started to unload into Astrid's mouth. She stopped bobbing immediately, but only increased her suction, her cheeks growing deep dimples. Kari kept pumping though, an evil smirk on her face as she grabbed a fistful of Astrid's hair and held her in place.

Every load you let out into Astrid's mouth was paired with a convulsion of her mouth as she swallowed it down until you had been thoroughly exhausted of resources.

Astrid kept sucking like a vacuum until it became clear there wasn't anything else on track for her stomach. Kari let her go pretty quickly after Astrid's cheeks filled with air again, and with a loud, wet pop, Astrid pulled off you.

"Whew… that was certainly something." Astrid gave a satisfied sigh and wiped some spit and smeared lipstick from her cheek with her sleeve.

"Told you he had stamina." Kari grumbled and gathered up her discarded clothes as she got to her feet.

"He lasted way longer than I'd thought but it's still over with plenty of time to spare." Astrid snorted and got to her feet.

Kari didn't respond, she just frowned, locked eyes with her friend and pointed to your still hard shaft.

"Well… shit." Astrid looked amused and shook her head.

"Told you we weren't getting off easy."

You gave an exaggerated chuckle to draw attention to the innuendo. Kari rolled her eyes however she was also fighting back a smile. Astrid was the exact opposite, showing her smile proudly, but subtly shaking her head at the stupid joke.

One thing you noticed however was neither girl seemed the slightest bit flirtatious anymore, in fact they just seemed tired.

"Well, can we at least get back to your place before you have your way with us again?" Astrid let out a sigh and looked at you in what you could only describe as disappointment.

"Not too excited to get pounded, huh?" You tried to sound sympathetic as you put your pants back on, but it was hard since you were still hard.

"Look, we said we wanted to talk with each other and we can't do that with a dick in our mouths, so don't do this again." Kari grunted, scowling at you, although to you it seemed forced and exaggerated.

"I can only promise I'll try." You winked at her.

"Best we can hope for I guess…."

"Neither of you seem particularly excited anymore." After that enthusiastic double blowjob it was hard not to notice the difference.

"That's 'cause we're not." Kari, still topless opened up the door to the cool outside and gestured for you to lead the way, "Astrid just wanted to try and get you off and this over with as soon as possible because she didn't believe my warnings."

On your way out you glanced at Astrid and raised an eyebrow. They must've been _really _good friends if they could agree on a plan to get you off with just a glance.

"Can you blame me? Not every day someone with a perpetual erection decides to take me home." Astrid shrugged and followed you out the door.

Despite how hot her complaints were, they were still quite obviously complaints, there was a distinct irritated bite to her voice, even if it wasn't particularly bad.

Maybe when you were done with them that would change. You still had an experiment to conduct. If you stuck to their lower two holes maybe you could make them feel good enough to change their opinions on you. Although, you weren't sure you could stay away from their mouths in their entirety for the entire night. Hell, you could always experiment some other time, you even had two other girls you could test with if it really came down to it.

"So where too?" Kari sighed and stretched, the cool night air already starting to harden her nipples.

Good question. It was beginning to get dark, you were just about out of cash, and your car was going to be packed with the two new additions. That being said, plenty of places would still be open for a while yet, you now had a working debit card, and you still had a trunk that was mostly empty.

Before anything else you had to get your new harem members into your car.

"My rides the shittiest one out this way." You pointed down the block.

You had to park pretty far away given all the cars on the street, but it wasn't so bad, it was peacefully quiet, once you made it a couple meters from the bar. The only sound was the gentle conversation between your two attractive companions, sprinkled in was some of their slightly drunk laughter. And while it was cool, even the topless Kari didn't seem too bothered. It was nearly a perfect evening…,

"Hey, you girls mind grabbing onto me while we walk?" The only problem was the forever-erection in your pants trying to get back in control, but you had the idea that giving orders and having human contact would be a decent enough band aid.

Astrid and Kari's cheerful chatter came to an abrupt stop and they locked gazes. For a moment you thought they were plotting places they could hide your body for daring to interrupt them again, but Kari broke the stalemate with a shrug. A moment later she pressing your arm between her breasts and hugging you tight.

"This something like what you want?" Kari looked up at you and tilted her head.

"Perfect." You smiled at her.

"'Least it's warmer." She mumbled while leaning her head against your arm and resuming her conversation with Astrid as if you hadn't interrupted.

Astrid unhesitatingly mimicked Kari, only being much taller, she was able to place her own head onto your shoulder.

Now it was a perfect evening.

The girls continued to gab and gossip, you weren't sure about what. It was all just background noise as your mind raced with ideas on how you wanted to play with your four new playthings. You were so distracted you almost walked past your own car, a shout from Kari was all that stopped you,

"What the hell are those?"

"Look, I already warned you it was shit." You found it was always painful when an attractive girl recoiled at the sight of your ride.

"Yeah, absolutely, but I meant your girlfriend. Her tit's are huge. Kari, keeping a firm grip on your arm literally dragged you closer to the passenger door so she could get a better look at Nalini.

Nalini looked just as surprised, only she looked embarrassed instead of awed. You also noted that her skirt was rolled up a little and one of the hand she had on her lap was 'mysteriously' soaked.

"Hah, yeah I wish, but she's already taken." You opened the passenger door as you explained.

"Welcome back sir... who are they? Girlfriend's?" Nalini gave a fake cough and rolled her skirt down a little bit more, giving a nervous glance towards Kari's bare chest.

You shook your head,

"Nalini, this is Astrid, and Kari," You gestured appropriately, "they're coming back with me since I'm such a valued customer." You paused for a laugh, or a snort, or something, but there was just smiles. Nalini for some reason seemed relieved.

Well, you had to assume you wouldn't have found your explanation all that absurd either if magic had altered your mind too.

"Astrid, Kari, this is Nalini, she's here to 'take the sting' out of some bank fees. In the back there is Emma--"

This time Kari cut you off with a snort as Emma waved lamely, her jaw hanging slightly slack at the sight of the two girls, or at least the topless one.

"There's another one…." Astrid gave an exaggerated gasp.

"The sting of bank fees? They hit you hard with overdrafts? Huh, big spender?" Kari broke away from you to tug playfully at the spoils you got from Olof.

You didn't want Astrid to find out the poster was free, you owed your new friend that much, so you blurted out the truth,

"Actually it was forty dollars to get my credit and debit cards replaced."

Kari immediately broke down into a fit of laughter, in her inebriated state she had to lean on you heavily for balance. Astrid even added in some chuckles of her own. Emma looked as confused as you felt, while Nalini was now looking away.

"It was twenty dollars each." You offered up your protest

"Yeah…. you got… you got taken for a ride!" Kari dropped to her knees and tried valiantly to rein in her laughter.

"It was set by the higher up's, there was nothing she could do." You were starting to feel that honoring Kari's wish to have her mouth free for the night was no longer something you cared for.

"That what she told you?" Kari's laughter had been pulled back into giggles, but she still couldn't compose herself properly.

"I bet." Astrid was far more composed, she was trying to smile through her grimace, "You get told there's outrageous fees, you raise a stink, and they just happen to be able to wave them for their _valued _customer. Bam, new favorite worker. Of course, you'd never find that at their competitors."

"Only you see mounds over here and just pay the damn thing." Kari wiped a tear from her eye, "I gotta admit that was pretty good." Kari tapped Nalini on the shoulder and grinned.

Nalini refused to look at any of you though.

You were drawing a blank on how to react. Anger, disappointment, betrayed, sad, everything just mixed together into a sickening white noise. It seemed so obvious now that it was spelled out to you, but in the moment, when you saw her tits and realized you could've had them you were blinded.

"Don't worry about it too much, I'm positive you're not the first guy she's taken to the cleaners." Kari gave you a couple hard pats on the back, "And I'm not just talking about at work. Eh, eh?" Kari gave Nalini a couple hard shoves, looking truly impressed.

Nalini still refused to look at you, she just coughed, her ears starting to go pink.

You made eye contact with Emma, who looked sorry for you for half a second before she looked away too.

"Just don't be too upset if he decides to give you a hard time for it." Kari gave Nalini one last firm pat on the shoulder before heading towards the back seat.

Astrid was quick to follow after her friend, shooting you a smirk, you wanted to believe it was sympathetic, but you couldn't shake the feeling that it was mocking, based on how you felt about yourself. Kari's comment brought you back to your senses though.

Yeah… you could be hard on her.

As you got into the driver's seat you were already cooking up ideas on how you were going to punish her. So she could really 'take the sting' out of those fees.

"Um, sir?" Nalini tentatively glanced up at you after you buckled in.

Your car turned over a bit before you finally got it going, yet another problem that comes with buying garbage even if that was all you could afford.

"Where… where are we heading to now?"

You kept your eyes on the road, the streets were quiet, but you didn't want to pull out without checking, just to be safe.

"I was just wondering if we could stop by my hotel. It's the giant yellow one on Main street. I mean if you have time. I just… I've got all my stuff there, and you said I'd be staying with you a month, and -- well I mean, I was thinking you probably don't want me wearing the same stuff for an entire month. I'd stink. Ha ha... I've also got some cute casual clothes that you might like to see me--"

"I'll think about it." You cut off her rambling with an icy grunt.

Nalini visibly winced but resumed looking at her hands. Kari started to cackle from the back seat, not helping your mood at all. Thankfully Astrid quickly thought to distract her with some more gossip about their shared past.

After several minutes of brooding you decided to break the silence in the front seat,

"For now, I don't think you need clothes."

"Oh, of course!" Nalini frantically undid her seat belt, tossed it to the side, and practically tore her clothes off.

Her shirt only had half its buttons to begin with, and in a moment it was tossed into the backseat,

"Oops! Sorry." Nalini stopped her stripping for a moment and winced.

"Don't worry about it." Kari pulling the shirt off her head and waved her hand flippantly, shoving the garment to the side before going back to listening to Astrid's gossip.

Next came Nalini's bra, with expert fingers she undid the clasps in a blink and tossed it behind her as well. This time conversation in the back stopped entirely as the bra hit Astrid in the face, where Kari immediately snatched it up and started laughing like she'd gone mad.

"This is fucking massive!" Kari bent over hysterical.

Astrid looked worn down and used to things, but Emma's face was a mixture of awe and concern for Kari.

Nalini had a bit of difficulty getting her skirt and panties down, but pushing herself up in her seat she managed it. She swung her arm around between the seats and tried to deposit the clothes a bit more gently, but the light weight and lacy underwear got enough distance to get Emma in the face.

Emma immediately started looking around nervously, luckily for her nobody cared even half as much as she obviously did.

"...I'm serious, after all these years he's still the same

asshole..." Astrid scoffed still completely engrossed in her own conversation.

"Emma?" You called out, the girl seemed terrified for a moment before she realized it was only you calling out to her, "How about you give those things a big whiff for me."

"...And he wonders why he can't keep a job or a girlfriend for more than a week…" Kari laughed, still paying attention to Astrid.

Emma was frozen for a moment, it was difficult to tell in the quick glances into your rearview mirror, but she looked as if her brain had been fried. And then you saw her bury her face into the fabric and take a deep snort, you were even able to hear it up front over your clunker's engine and in a short lull in Astrid and Kari's conversation.

"Oh and don't be afraid to itch the ditch, that goes for all of you."

"...Hey where'd 'Max Stamina' pick you up from anyways?" Kari didn't seem to hear you, or if she did, didn't care.

"Uh…." Emma tensed up, panties jammed in her face,

and one hand making its way into her pants, looking just as nervous as a girl who'd been caught sniffing panties and getting ready to masturbate.

"What about my stockings and shoes, sir?" Nalini still seemed nervous around you, she spoke gently, barely above a whisper.

Despite her gentle tone all you could think when reminded of her existence was how she wronged you.

"Lose 'em. You won't need them. From now on, while you're serving me, you don't get to walk. I want you to crawl everywhere."

"Cert -- certainly sir." Nalini choked on her own spit when she answered, but she didn't hesitate to comply.

"Yeah, don't worry, if you've got a job to do go on." Astrid's beautiful voice cooed, strangely motherly.

Your attention returning to the backseat, or at least as much as you could spare, you saw Astrid, one hand resting on Emma's wrist the other gesturing towards the younger girl's crotch.

"Um… Thanks…." Emma gave a nervous chuckle and quickly stuffed her hand the full way down her pants and let out a satisfied moan, while trying to inhale Nalini's panties.

"So for a first job, how're you liking it?" Astrid changed gears pretty quickly, in perturbed by Emma's panty sniffing or jilling off at your okay.

"I know my first job wasn't nearly as laid back as a grocery store…" Kari, likewise, just gave her own anecdote of her own, untroubled by the girl masturbating beside her.

"…Yeah, it's not too bad…" Emma was starting to find her stride but you noticed she was making more than a few poorly concealed glances towards Kari's bare chest.

You were a little disappointed that Kari and Astrid didn't seem to want to put on a show for you, not that you could particularly enjoy it at the moment, but it did make sense in a way. Just because your wallet had convinced them that sex was a service they offered, didn't mean they had to give good service. Which brought you back to the devoted bank manager currently stuffing her rolled up stockings into her shoes for safe keeping.

"Glasses too, and that bun while you're at it." You glanced at her sideways.

You were still hurting because of her manipulations, but being a difficult customer didn't seem to be hurting her as much as you'd hoped.

"Of course." Nalini chuckled nervously, "They're just read glasses anyways." She then deposited the spectacles into a cup holder before working some magic on the chopsticks in her hair.

As soon as she was done the conversation in the back seat transformed into awestruck gasps and appreciative compliments.

You yourself actually took your eyes off the road for a moment to admire Nalini's incredibly long, silky hair cascade down her shoulders like an obsidian waterfall to rest around her ass. She took off her angular glasses and shook her thick hair out with a glamorous shake of her head, making sure she had everything loose.

The transformation was remarkable. She looked sexy before, but now she was gorgeous. The care that went into her hair was far more apparent. Instead of looking stuffy, albeit sexy, she looked far more free spirited and fun. You actually felt a little bit of pride at managing to snap her up, but you still couldn't let her off with scamming you completely scot free.

You had to think of something that could hurt her as much as she hurt you. She seemed a bit shocked at being told to crawl everywhere, maybe you could build on that somehow? Pet play might weird her out? Or maybe just general humiliation? What would a woman as put together as her hate?

"Hey, Nalini, are you on birth control?"

"...Yeah... why?" Nalini started to wring her hands as if she could already see where you were going with things.

"What would you say if I told you to stop while I keep you?"

"...Oh! I... I guess I could do that...." She kept her eyes locked straight ahead, her face was beginning to pale, and you were pretty sure she was starting to breathe a bit quicker, but you couldn't be sure since you were still focusing on not running into a ditch.

Surprisingly, your loins were only now beginning to stir,

it seems the shame of being manipulated outweighed even magic, but now you had a guaranteed way out of your shameful defeat….

"Hah! Not me. My job's not worth that shit!" Kari giggled in the back seat.

"I don't have any birth control….." Emma squeaked, pulling her hand out of her pants, no longer looking to pleasure herself, instead she was nervously wringing Nalini's panties.

"Oof," Astrid gave Emma a sympathetic pat on the back, "that's rough. You should really make sure you're in control of that, no guarantee a customer's going to use a condom for your sake."

You had to pay special attention to the road as things started to wind back and forth, but you could feel eyes boring into the back of your head.

"By the way, Astrid, Kari, I was wondering what gets you hot and bothered?" You suddenly remembered your conversation on the way up to the bar, and your whole plan to see if you could get everyone to like you, or rather like fucking you.

You had enough of them now that you could probably

pick and choose who you wanted to be nicest to, just based on who would be easiest to please. Nalini was already going to be yours for a month and you even had a perfect excuse to be mean to her for a bit, so she was teetering pretty hard but it might depend on what Kari and Astrid had to say.

"You mean what gets me off?" Kari rhetorically asked for clarification, not waiting for an answer, "I like a guy with balls. Too many pussy's show at work, try to hit on me, and piss their pants when I don't drop to my knees and blow them right away."

"Oh, so you like it when a guy makes you blow them?" You put a dark menace into your voice.

Kari responded by cackling like mad,

"Oh, I dare you to try and break me. I'd love to see that."

A quick glance in the mirror showed a smile on her face that told you she meant every word of it.

After a few moments of silence you prodded the next girl,

"Astrid?"

After a heavy sigh she finally responded

"Look, I appreciate your patronage, but I'm not here to play with you. Just pick a hole and have your fun. " Astrid brushed you off, not exactly upset, but showing just how little she cared about you taking her home to play with.

"Aww, and after everything I bought?" You pretended to sound hurt.

"Look, just because you bought some expensive merch doesn't mean it wasn't stuff that didn't have me half naked on them. No offense, but I didn't pose for those expecting upstanding people to buy them, so you'll have to forgive me if I'm not impressed even if you spent a couple hundred." She ended with a dissatisfied huff.

Everyone in the care was silent for a good length of time. You eventually decided to break the silence.

"So I guess you're telling me you have a no refund policy, huh?"

All the girls in the car gave a chuckle at that, although Nalini and Emma didn't have nearly as much energy as the inebriated Astrid and Kari.

"I think you'll just have to experiment with her." Kari jostled your seat a little bit as she came down for her laughter.

It earned her an attempted punch for Astrid, but she squeezed out of the way and it just humored her even more.

The girls in the backseat kept up their conversation the whole way, there seemed to be no end to the topics they could cover, bouncing from one to another, barely ten seconds could go by without them having something new to add. Nalini however was busy staring at her knees, not a single trace of her usual attempts at showing a friendly face.

Even if her smiles were usually fake you never got the sense that they were particularly forced, so her new despondence was palpable. Considering she had scammed you while you were strapped for cash though, you couldn't deny the deliciousness of it in its own perverse way.

In the end, Nalini didn't say a word the rest if the trip, not even when you pulled to a stop in front of her hotel.

Even based on her vague description of 'giant and yellow on main street,' it was a cinch to actually find the building. You had come to your decision after you finally figured out something that made her squirm, so you decided to throw your new dog a bone instead of a boner.

The girls in the back finally fell silent though, and looked at you curiously.

"Alright ladies, you don't have to come with me, but Nalini and I are going to be gone a minute. Oh! And make sure you don't come without me." You chuckled at the absurdity of the statement in general.

The girls, minus Nalini, all groaned. Kari shot you a playful string of drunken curses for daring to make such a shitty joke.

To your immense pleasure, Nalini joined you on the way to the front door on all fours. She was refusing to look anywhere but the asphalt, and with her hands busy supporting herself she had to carry her purse in her teeth.

It was slow goings since you didn't want to outpace her and Nalini had to stop quite frequently to shake off a rock or other bits of debris with a muffled wince, but it was glorious having this kind of power over her. Admittedly, it was power she had granted you with her determination to be professional, but you could still take advantage regardless.

You opened the door for Nalini and followed in after her, just as an elderly gentleman waved his good-byes to the receptionist and headed straight for you.

The man barely made it two steps towards you before he slowed down, his eyes dropped to the fully nude, incredibly well endowed woman crawling on the ground, then up to you, his face was blank. A half step later a change came over him, and he resumed her prior gait, even giving you a friendly nod and a good day to Nalini before he walked past you.

The receptionist had a similar reaction. The second she saw you she looked confused, a little shocked even, but the next second she had a smile on her face, the scene no longer fazing her, or if it was she didn't show it.

Once you both reached the counter, without even asking you, Nalini got onto her knees, spit out her purse and started to root through it.

"Good evening! Is there anything I can help you with, ma'am?" The woman behind the counter leaned over to give a warm smile down at Nalini, and gave you a curious glance over.

"Ah, yeah, actually, I'm going to be checking out tonight, if that's possible." Nalini withdrew her key card from her purse and presented it.

"I can certainly do that. Was there something wrong with your stay?" The woman took the card from Nalini and started tapping away at her computer.

"No, it was fine. Something just came up with my job, so I won't needing my room anymore."

"Ah!" The woman at the counter nodded slowly, her gaze flicking over to you for a second before she leaned away from her computer and towards Nalini, "Now before I deactivate your key, I noticed you didn't come from your room…."

"Right!" Nalini yelped, finally showing some signs of energy, even looking at you for a moment before deflating again, "I need to get my stuff together. Can't believe I forgot."

"Rough day at work?" The woman smiled.

Nalini glanced at you hesitantly before nodding,

"Rough next few weeks actually. My fault entirely, but…."

"Say no more. I don't think I've ever had any job that didn't stress me loopy every now and again." The woman chuckled, gestured at her computer then handed back the key card and waved you and Nalini off.

You had no idea what was running through the receptionist's mind throughout the entire conversation, but the second Nalini said she brought her own fate onto herself the woman seemed friendlier, even shooting you a friendly smile before you left.

If you really thought about it though the reactions of people you weren't paying could actually be pretty interesting to play around with. The receptionist wasn't under your control in anyway, Nalini was the one that paid for the room before you even met her, but she had to have at least acknowledged what you were putting Nalini through considering she hadn't been particularly welcoming initially.

There were a lot of thing's that you could play around with, and this was yet another you'd have to consider. That would have to wait for at least a little bit longer though.

Now that you were inside the hotel Nalini was able to move at a much brisker pace without various debris getting in the way, it was to both your luck that Nalini's room was only halfway down the first floor hallway.

You let Nalini lead the way, more than happy to stroll behind her given the view. Once she made it to her room, she opened the door and crawled in.

The room itself was a mess. it was small, with just a single queen sized mattress dominating most of the space, but everywhere that was free now had an article of clothing scattered across it, there were also two sizable suitcases were on opposite sides of the bed.

"Tornado came through here, huh?"

"Oh, yeah, sorry." Nalini was devoid of all emotion, "Do you mind if I stand while I get my things together." She looked up at you with a frown.

You took a moment to consider it, it wouuuuuuuuuuuld be hot to see her crawl around a bit more, but just about anything she did while naked would be hot, and you did want to get home at some point and actually have a party, so you gave her the okay,

"Only until you're packed though." You gave a firm stipulation, "I can take care of your bags afterwards."

"Thank you, sir." There wasn't even an attempt at refusing, even for the sake of politeness.

You would've chalked it up to practicality, she couldn't haul luggage and crawl, but up until now she seemed to be doing her best to be professional and cordial, but now there was a distinct lack of effort. She even seemed to be packing things as slowly as she could.

Your eyes dropped to the floor as you considered what this meant. She must've really hated the idea of risking a kid with a random stranger who showed up at her new job. In a fucked up way though, she deserved it, hell, she herself admitted she did a few minutes earlier.

As you considered the facts and your own personal opinions on the matter your eyes fell on a snow white scrap of fabric on the ground. You picked it up and it revealed it was little more than a folded napkin and dental floss. It was a tiny white thong, it was smooth as silk and opaque, but you had a hard time imagining that there was enough of it there to give any decent coverage.

"You must really not want me to put a kid into you." You decided to break the silence as you twirled your new find around a finger.

Nalini jumped at your voice, and physically recoiled when she saw you playing with her panties, there was only a minimal attempt to hide her horror,

"Not at all sir, it's part of my job."

You weren't buying that for a second, she barely even tried to hide the defeat in her voice.

"You're not going to try and make me pay child support as revenge if I knock you up, are you?"

Of course, it was a logical leap, a legitimate obstacle that should've had you hesitant to even consider going through with your scheme, but the second the thought entered your mind you were filled with an overwhelming certainty that things would work out.

The best you could explain it was every fibre of your being knew it as a fact, it was as real as 'you needed air to live,' you didn't know how, you just knew that if you chose to knock someone up, everything would 'work out.' It was a sensation reminiscent of when you first suffered withdrawal and just knew you had to get some pussy to relieve your overwhelming pain and lust. You could only assuming your magic sex granting wallet had an affect, it seemed to make as much sense as anything else dictating your life the past couple days.

Nalini didn't have your wallet though, and you were positive she didn't have the same certainty, proven by a flash of realization across her face. She had an out now, she could try and manipulate you some more and convince you that knocking her up would be dangerous to your meagre bank account. She deflated before she spoke though, looking even more defeated than before,

"I'm pretty sure a baby would be covered by workers comp." She chose professionalism over self preservation.

It was impossible for you to hate her any longer. The woman was literally going to let you knock her up for your own pleasure and let you run off. All in all, forty dollars was nothing compared to that, even if by all rights it should've been closer to four. You had only wanted to see her squirm before, but you were seriously considering going through with it now.

"Still not a fan of having a bun in the oven though?" Having empathy for her kind of made you feel disgusted in your own desires though.

"Like I said --"

"I'm asking you a question!" You stopped twirling the

thong and mustered up the most dominating tone of voice you could. You needed an honest answer.

Nalini was taken aback, stopping her slow, methodical folding and looked at you in shock.

"There's no need to shout sir."

"There is when you won't give me an honest answer. If I wanted bullshit I'd ask for it."

Nalini chewed her lip for a moment, then met your gaze with a soft, yet confident one of her own,

"I wouldn't mind starting a family, honestly. A child… even with a customer doesn't seem so bad. I'm sure my fiancé wouldn't mind either. He understands how important my job is." Nalini stopped and looked to the ground. Searching for something.

"But…?" You tried to push her.

Even if you were positive things would 'work out,' logically you couldn't know if it was just for you, or if you'd be ruining some budding families life with your own lust. Part of you didn't care. You had the base, animal desire to spread your genes and knock someone up, even if logic told you it was a much more complex issue. Your wallet was trying to nudge you over to being an asshole, it had to be. You might not have been a perfect person before, but you weren't sub-human scum. The devil on the wallet reminded you of stories where demonic pacts were double edged swords. Of course, maybe you weren't being altered by magic but even then you were reminded of the adage, 'absolute power corrupts absolutely.'

"But, I think it's a little early in my life to be raising a kid. I mean, my fiancé is still in school, and my job forces me to move around so much. I wouldn't be able to give my child a good home."

"So you're worried about raising my child right more than how it'll affect your life?" Despite your disgust in yourself, there was an indescribable thrill of emphasizing that it would be your spawn inside her.

"I mean, a child's a big step in general, so it's scary I guess." Nalini didn't even flinch, she instead started collecting her clothes again, "But, I don't think I'd ever be personally ready for that kind of responsibility, I think the only way would be to just take the plunge, y'know? But yeah, I'm mostly worried about doing the bare minimum for our kid." She laughed nervously, a short hollow chuckle, and gripped the shirt she was holding tightly.

You couldn't help but fixate on one part though; 'our kid.' Perhaps she thought you were giving her a cue, or maybe she was already convinced you had decided to knock her up and was simply being factual, either way you weren't going to stop yourself now. You dropped your pants, the noise of fabric hitting the ground and your belt buckle clacking stunned her as she looked at you with a mixture of panic and confusion.

"Keep packing, I'd like to get out of here soon." You grunted and wrapped her soft thong around your pole as best you could, given what you had to work with.

Nalini looked relieved, but still a little apprehensive as she watched you pump your meat.

"Uh, yes, sir."

Nalini had finished packing one of her suitcases and pushed it to the side, lifting the other one onto the bed. She unzipped the package but then slowly turned to you,

"Do I really have to stop taking my birth control." She gave you this heart wrenching pleading look. One only an attractive naked woman could give.

"You saw my bank account and you still decided to rip me a new one." Your empathy for her was starting to fade at the mere memory however.

"Look, I didn't want to say this in front of a customer, but I'm only taking my birth control to get my periods under control. They're pretty bad."

You stopped jerking and tossed the thong onto the bed, then approached her with a sly grin,

"I'm sure you'll want to get pregnant as fast as possible then, right?"

Nalini looked destroyed. To your slight shame that just made you even harder. You wanted revenge and it seemed like this was the best kind, but you didn't want to be a monster, you just wanted to tease her a bit. This seemed to be going too far though. She seemed to be fighting back tears. You could hardly imagine wanting or even needing a job this badly.

You felt kind of bad, but were too stunned to fully piece together a proper way to salvage things, but you had to say something.

"I'm pretty sure birth control just tricks your body into thinking it's already pregnant, doesn't it?" You were somewhat upset that that was the best you could come up with, but maybe a question would buy you time to think of something better.

Except, a visible change came over Nalini. For a moment she didn't seem to be entirely present, but then a hand flew up to her mouth, then she let out a slightly muffled squeal,

"I'm an absolute idiot." She fixed you with a wide eyed stare, her hand dropping down to her chest and she started to chuckle ruefully, "I can't believe I didn't realize that."

She sucked on her lips and shook her head slowly, her ears turning pink.

"We all have brain farts from time to time, don't worry about it." You gave your own relieve scoff. You had been certain you were pushing her too far, it was nice to know it was because her mind was actually somewhere else.

But seeing her nearly cry at the very idea of carrying your child had gotten you hornier than you liked to admit and you needed to get off yet again.

"I'm so sorry you had to see that. I can't believe how

stupid I was. I even started talking about my period, and I doubt you wanted to hear about that." Nalini ran a hand through her hair as she started to laugh nervously.

The pregnancy was a complete non-issue to her now. Kari had flat out told you knocking her up was off the table, but Nalini was more worried about refusing you than actually getting a bun in the oven. That sunk it. You put an abrupt stop to her self depreciative laughter when you grabbed her around the waist and tipped her onto the bed. After letting out a squeal she looked up at you in surprise,

"Ahh! Already? I mean, I just took one of my pills this morning, it's going to take a bit more --"

You were barely listening though, you practically leaped on top of her, and straddled her stomach, laying your pipe between her impressive tits.

"I think it's about time I finally give these puppies a try."

"Oh~." Nalini drew out the syllable and gave you a knowing grin, "Well, I'm actually surprised you took so long to give them a go." She cupped her breasts and squeezed them together, seeming like her old self all over again, all though perhaps a little more genuinely friendly now that you had seen her in such a vulnerable state, "Most guys want to go for a good ol' boob job before anything else."

You let out an appreciative moan the second her mounds enveloped you,

"Sounded like you hate titjobs." It took everything you had to speak in complete thoughts as you started to rock your hips back and forth.

"Are you kidding? I love them! My tits are one of my best features! Just, I like it when they're not my only feature." Nalini beamed up at you and started to work her tits in opposite directions.

You only vaguely registered what she was saying, her soft breasts enveloped your meat and mind in tandem. Every inch of you was lost into her soft pillowy depths. Or so you thought.

"Well hello there big boy." Nalini giggled and grinned up at you.

A moment later she stopped moving her breasts, stuck out her tongue, and leaned towards her chest. Every thrust afterwards you felt the tip of your cock brush against her tongue. She began to make a game out of giving you a flick of her tongue every time your tip came close. Her timing was off more often than not, but seeing her hungrily licking at the tip of your meat just barely poking through the top of her impressive chest was amazing.

Every failed flicked that didn't manage to make decent contact seemed to amuse her, coaxing an occasional chuckle and a warm smile that told you she was miraculously back to normal.

You pushed yourself as deep into her mounds as you could, smooshing them up against your balls and sunk your hand soft flesh. Nalini gasped, and then mewled appreciatively at the firm, yet controlled pressure and switch up her own tactics without hesitation. With the extra inch you managed to push through her tits she managed to wrap her lips around the tip of your cock. She wasn't even able to get your entire head into her mouth, but she sucked hard while moving one hand from her breast down to your balls.

You were filled with a sensation you could only describe as, she was trying to suck your dick inside out, not that you were going to complain. There was something amazing about putting all she could into the very tip of your dick while tickling your balls with the tip of her fingers, it sent a tingle down your cock and up your spine.

Your were being consumed by pleasure, your desire to move or even breath had left you almost entirely, and you let out an animal groan with what little air you had to show your appreciation. Nalini seemed encouraged by the noise, her suction, somehow increasing further, her tongue snaking forwards to probe around the end of your cock. Her fingers traced gently around the outline of your balls, sending another violent shiver up your spine, one that manifested in a short physical spasm and an even shorter, jittery grunt.

Nalini stopped sucking entirely, just for a moment to let out a staccato chuckle, with your dick still planted in her mouth you felt the laugh more than you heard it. A beat later she was sucking like a vacuum again, and moved her hands on top of yours and gently pet the back of your hands.

You managed to regain enough of your senses to at least consider what she meant by the gesture. You couldn't be sure, but you had an idea and slid each hand to the side, cupping her breasts gently and flicked your thumbs across her nipples.

Nalini's reaction was instantaneous. Her eyes went wide, suction started to falter, and her gentle probing with her tongue had stopped and been replaced by a forceful swirling of her tongue around the end of your meat.

It was difficult to place whether having her falter helped give you access to more faculties, or just the idea of making her squirm spurred you on, probably a bit of both, but you finally had a solid thought and pinched her nipples between your thumb and forefingers.

Nalini let out a purr and immediately moved her soft, warm hands on top of yours to help you support her heavy breasts.

You tweaked her nipples like you were tuning a radio.

"Mm-hm-hm-hmmm." Nalini let out another muffled chuckle, this time much more audibly, but still refusing to let you out of her mouth. However, now she was having some trouble sucking your brain cells out through your dick.

Pressing your advantage you pressed her rapidly hardening nipples into your index fingers and slowly rubbed them from bottom to top with your thumbs, repeatedly. Every time Nalini arched her back under you, ever so slightly, and there was an immediate increase in her suction rather than a falter.

"That… that's it." You only now started to realize just how little you had been breathing, "I want to cream -- all over your face."

You stopped teasing her and instead squeezed her breasts together, creating a tight cavity and started to thrust with purpose. The very moment you pulled free from Nalini's mouth your were met with a satisfying smack as she had clearly not been expecting you to pull out so suddenly.

"You don't… want to cum in me?" Nalini was almost shorter of breath than you were, it made simple question sound like she was disappointed.

You were pretty sure she wasn't but were stilled encouraged by it.

"You promised me a month." You began to lose yourself as you started to increase your speed even more, "I'll knock you up yet."

Nalini didn't answer, instead she closed her eyes, and squeezed her mouth shut. She didn't look upset, merely waiting for your loads.

It only took a few more frantic thrusts and you did just that and began painting her face. Your mind instantly exploded into white, senseless ecstasy and your veins seemed to fill with electricity as you shot a couple ropes into her silky hair. You readjusted down to her forehead, coating her brow. You got one of her cheeks with a long rope just under her eye, and covered her other cheek with a sticky coat of its own. Finally when you started to near the end of your orgasm you squeezed out the last, generous bit right over her lips. Once you were exhausted you gave her mouth a couple satisfied taps with your slowly softening meat and began to get off of her.

"Get your things together, I want to get you back home sometime soon." You sighed, finally satisfied, for a moment at least, "And don't be afraid to forget your birth control. I've decided you won't be needing it."

Nalini flicked her tongue out of her mouth and lapped up any cum she could before she slowly opened her eyes testingly.

"I can do that, sir." Nalini smiled at your warmly through her mask of cum, "Does this mean I shouldn't clean up?"

It took maybe a second for you to decide,

"No, you're crawling out like that."

"Yes, sir." Nalini hesitated for a second but then gave you a confident nod before setting out to gather the rest of her things together.

A moment later, when she had flipped open her second suitcase, you were met with an interesting sight of a long, thin, silver vibrator tucked poorly away into a pocket on the inside of the bag. Nalini didn't seem to notice it hanging out of its pocket though, she kept folding clothes and stuffing them into her suitcase, far faster than she had before. She did notice once you snapped it up however.

"Oh god!" For some reason, her reaction was embarrassment, she moved to grab her cum covered face, but seemed to think better of it at the last second, "Give that back!" She reached out for it as fast as she could.

You were just a little bit faster though, stretching it out of reach and holding her weak efforts of protest back with one hand.

"Well, I didn't know you came with accessories." You were genuinely pleased at this new development, "This could be a lot of fun for later."

Something about what you said managed to calm Nalini down, she was still red from what you could see under her facial.

"What other toys you got?" You tried to tease her, waggling the vibrator menacingly as she resumed packing.

"Just a some vibrating bullets and a couple dildos." Nalini cleared her throat, still obviously a little embarrassed, but recovering shockingly quickly.

Maybe you had planted it in her mind that you hadn't merely stumbled upon embarrassing sex toys, rather you actually just discovered a new faucet for her services.

"A 'couple' dildos?" You were confused by the superfluous amount of toys.

She already had a vibrator, why did she need anything else? Even if she got tired of vibrations for whatever reason, she could turn it off, right?

"Sometime's I'm in the mood for the big one, sometimes the small one." Nalini shrugged, no longer the least bit fazed.

It seemed somewhat plausible to you. Granted, as a man you weren't nearly as socially free to buy toys so you had a hard time imagining that things could differ much from one toy to another, but as a practical human being it seemed that it was a lot to bring on a business trip. Maybe that was why she was embarrassed? In the end, you could at the very least appreciate that Nalini came with a decent stock of tools for you plans.

This had been an amazing detour.

You'd tried to be practical, you held off on as much instant gratification as you could, in the idea of a bigger pay out later. It was finally time to cash out. You had four girls at your disposal, and it seemed clear to you now that there really wasn't anything they wouldn't let you do to them.

"Open wide." With a fiendish grin you wiggled the vibrator at Nalini.

She had just zipped up her second suitcase, the last of her things packed away, and was already starting to bend at the knee, looking to you for approval, but at your command her face transformed into confusion. Her eyes flicked down towards the vibrator, for a moment she seemed unsure, but then slowly leaned forward and wordlessly opened her mouth.

You pushed the silver toy into her mouth then squeezed her cheeks,

"Suck it. And make it messy." Your grin got wider and you let the girl go with a gentle pat on the cheek.

The mere idea that she was as much a toy to you as the vibrator was to her was impossible to resist. It seemed only right you played with them together, at least for a little bit.

Nalini looked more confused still. You didn't give her much time to think though, you were already starting to work the toy towards her throat. She winced momentarily as you felt the toy meet some resistance, but she quickly relaxed her throat to let the intruder in. Once your fingers were inches from her lips you slowly pulled the toy back out, stopping just before it was free from her lips.

Nalini inhaled deeply as soon as her throat was free, then started sucking the toy, her confusion replaced with determination as you began pumping the silver rod in and out of her throat. Following your demands, she made sure there was plenty of spit, after a minute her chin was covered in drool and the vibrator was thoroughly drenched.

"That was fun, but we should go now."

Having her blow her own vibrator was fun, but you didn't want to keep the rest of your girls waiting any longer. When you removed the vibrator from Nalini's mouth, void of any warning,her head bobbed forward just a touch, giving the impression that she was eager to suck on it some more.

"Was… that it?" Nalini swallowed as much spit as she could, now that she didn't need it anymore, and looked at you apprehensively.

You traced a wet line around one of her nipples with the tip of the vibrator,

"For now." You were nearly bursting with excitement.

Nalini seemed to be the one having difficulty keeping her composure now though. You could see a wet trail going down the inside of her thighs. Part of it was left over from the fun you had before, but you certainly weren't helping her calm down now.

During your ministrations you accidentally brought the toy roaring to life. In your shock it almost slipped from your fingers and you ended up pushing it into Nalini's hardened nipple.

Nalini's reaction was quite a bit faster than yours; her eyes shot open and her back straightened noticeably, then her entire posture relaxed, her eyes fluttered back down into a dreamy far away look and she sucked in her lips. A beat later you flicked your thumb back across the switch.

"That's enough of this. On the ground, we're heading

back to my place."

"Of course." She sounded a little disappointed, but smiled all the same.

As Nalini got to her knees you mentioned that you just had to put the vibrator away first. Nalini looked back up with you and nodded her understanding, then waited patiently like a good dog.

It seemed like a shame to put the messy toy in with her clothes though….

Without a word of warning you leaned over and traced her backdoor with the spit soaked silver toy.

Nalini squeaked and shuffled forward a half step, then looked back at you,

"Excuse me," Nalini hung her head solemnly, "you just surprised me."

"Sit still." You simple response was punctuated by a hard slap across one of her cheeks then giving it a hard squeeze.

Nalini, still recovering from your slap nodded mutely, a grimace on her face.

Using her cheek as a makeshift grip, you coaxed her to lean back towards you and slowly worked the drenched vibrator into her hole.

You were met with some initial resistance, but after you got the tip inside, Nalini exhaled slowly, her hole relaxed and the rest of the toy slipped in with ease. You kept pushing until you were a little fearful you might lose it if you went any farther.

Now that you thought about it, you did remember Nalini mentioning her fiancé was a fan of anal. Maybe she was too considering how easy it was though.

"Is that all, sir?" Nalini exhaled deeply one last time and smiled back you, far from bothered by her cum facial or even the new anal intrusion.

Then you flicked the vibrator onto high.

"Oh god! What the fu--" Nalini slapped a hand over her mouth and collapsed to the ground with her ass in the air.

She continued letting out a low groan and met your eyes with what you assume was a glare. Being upset with you would be appropriate, but she seemed to be having difficulty keeping a straight face.

It was a far more violent reaction than you had expected. Both from the toy and Nalini. You had accidentally flicked the sliding switch to medium before, and it sounded like a reasonable toy, now it sounded like a piece of industrial machinery.

"You certainly picked a quality product." You laughed and sheepishly toned the device down.

You tried low, and you could barely hear it, buried in her ass as it was, but based on the vibrations you felt low would probably be more than enough for her own pleasure. But for your pleasure you kept it a bit closer to the middle.

Once you straightened back up and it was clear you weren't going to put the device any lower Nalini gave you big, wet puppy dog eyes and let out a pitiful moan. It was difficult for you to muster any pity when you gazed at her glazed face however. Just looking at her actually made you want to torment her in all sorts of other fun ways.

"Alright, come along girl" That would have to wait just a tad bit longer though.

Nalini let out one more pitiful groan, then with shaky

limbs followed after you as you dragged her things out with you.

It was pretty quiet, save for the soft buzzing come from Nalini's tail, so you didn't run into anyone on the way into the lobby.

You were equal parts nervous and excited. You still didn't have much experience taking your fun public. Reactions so far seemed to point towards being able to do whatever the fuck you wanted, but a sensible part of you was still expecting people to throw a fit.

"Oh my. This one's really putting you through the ringer isn't he?" The receptionist was wide eyed, but that was just her emoting before she smiled warmly.

Nalini shrugged as best she could and kept crawling.

You kept your mouth shut, frankly a little nervous about accidentally bursting your own bubble.

As you and Nalini neared the desk you stopped rolling the suitcases and a very audible buzzing cut through the silence. The receptionist looked around curiously for a bit, then her eyes met with Nalini who jerked her head backwards. The woman at the counter leaned over it a bit and then realization struck, and she started to laugh.

"Oh dear, I'm so sorry for you." The woman accepted Nalini's key card again, then shook her head slowly, a smile still on her face, but her glances at you rubbed you the wrong way.

"In my defence I'm just getting my money's worth." You felt she was judging you so you brought up the bank card debacle and you could see the woman's respect for Nalini die, just a tiny bit.

Nalini didn't see anything though, because even if she was kneeling to deal with the receptionist, she was hanging her head in shame.

"It's not all bad though, I mean, forty dollars is kind of brutal, but she's got some crazy good customer care."

"Forty dollar good?" The woman smirked as she put the final touches on whatever she was doing to the key card.

You looked down at Nalini, naked, cum covering her face, and vibrator drilled up her ass, looking up at you apprehensively.

"Absolutely."

Both girls seemed surprised by the answer, the receptionist leaned a bit more to impressed though.

"The question should be whether her service is as good for, I don't know, a nine hundred percent hike? Does ten times the price sound about right?"

Nalini went back to looking hurt, opting to stay silent. The receptionist laughed however,

"Yeah, I can imagine that's pretty hard to live up too. But poor girl seems to be doing her hardest, right?"

Nalini frantically nodded and opened her mouth to say something, but you silenced her with a look. You weren't even trying too, but she withered instantly.

"Well, I'd say she's getting there, but it takes more than lip service to get away with robbery."

"Ah, well, you've got a point there." The receptionist nodded sympathetically.

"I'd say she was asking for it though. You don't try something like that unless you're prepared to go balls deep." To your surprise you weren't the only one to laugh at your own double entendre.

As you and the receptionist shared a chuckle you looked down at Nalini, who had returned to her hands and knees now that her business was through, and you were struck by an idea.

"If you were in my position, how would you make her work off her offense?"

The woman blinked at you a few times then exhaled slowly,

"Ooh boy, you mean, like…" She started snapping her fingers, then with a wince said, "sex her up? Pardon my French."

"Essentially." You did your best to assuage the woman's guilt at talking like that in front of you, "I mean, she needs to work this off somehow, y'know?"

"Right… well…." The woman completely recovered leaned back in her chair and put a hand to her chin.

Nalini was starting to shift nervously on the spot, she couldn't see above the counter, but she glanced up at you a few times and wiggled her butt every now and then, the vibrator no doubt starting to really get to her.

"If I was you" She put heavy emphasis on the 'you', "I'd

probably try to have as much sex as possible to make the price worth it."

You smiled pretty widely at that.

"But that would probably be a bit on the nose though. Besides, she could enjoy that too or even act like a drugged mattress for the whole thing, yeah? I suppose I, or I mean, you, would probably want her to put in as much effort as possible, right? So maybe a lot of strict orders would be something to consider."

"Too strict and she might not want to follow them though." You were starting to hit your stride with interacting with people while having deviant adventures.

It might've helped that it was quiet and with only one other person around, or maybe it was just having such a natural conversation partner, but you didn't hesitate to kneel down and give Nalini a good spank to emphasize your concerns that she might disobey.

"Riiiiight." The woman clapped herself on the forehead as she leaned over the counter to watch you, "I'm really bad at this stuff, I don't know what to tell you." She gave a wry chuckle, "I guess maybe keep doing stuff like that," She wiggled her finger at Nalini's head, "like, for revenge."

"Humiliate her?" You smiled and toyed with the vibrator in Nalini's ass a little, causing her arms to shake under her.

"Yeah, just take her out with you in public and parade her around. Treat her like she isn't a person." The receptionist smiled at you, then a moment later her face fell, "Uh, sorry." She winced at Nalini.

"It doesn't matter. I promise." Nalini smiled back weakly as you gave her ass a firm squeeze.

You were already getting a few ideas.

"You've given me some good advice." You gave Nalini one last spank, turned her vibrator up just a tiny bit, and nodded at the receptionist.

"Glad I could help." The receptionist shrugged and chuckled.

You said your goodbye's and waved for Nalini to follow you as you dragged her luggage along.

You happily marched along back to your ride, leaving

Nalini in the dust. She was even slower on the trip back, but you had luggage to deal with.

You popped the trunk and were met with the sight of groceries. You'd forgotten about that. But looking back at Nalini making her way towards you, a look of wavering determination on her cum coated face, and the three girls laughing in the back seat, you couldn't really beat yourself up too much. Anyone would forgot if they were in your situation.

You moved the bags out of the way, hoping nothing had gone bad after how long you left them out, then plunked in the luggage and went around to the drivers side to wait for Nalini.

As soon as you opened the door you heard Astrid say,

"I can understand why some would have the hots for them, but if you spend more than a couple hours day around them all together you'd cool down real fast." In her hands was the poster you'd bought and all three girls were looking it over.

"You don't like your band mates?" You raised an eyebrow before turning around and taking your seat as Nalini crawled her way around the front of the car.

"I like them fine. I just don't want to fuck them." Astrid shot you a withering glare like it was the most obvious thing in the world, then added, in neutral tone "This one wanted to know how big of a slut I was." She jabbed Emma in the shoulder.

"Wha -- no! I didn't --!" Emma, Nalini's panties still grasped tight, looked mortified.

"She's kidding." Kari shook her head and smiled, "She's actually proud of how slutty she is."

"Oh, fuck you!" Astrid's scowl did a poor job of hiding her smile.

Kari responded with a cartoonist chuckle.

Astrid couldn't fight her own smirk, and changed the subject,

"Seriously, it feel's like babysitting most of the time. I mean I literally walked in on Olof eating paste once while the others cheered him on."

Before you could hear the rest of the thought Nalini was opening the passenger door.

"Oh! Actually, could you switch spots with Emma?" It

was little more than a whim, but if you thought about it, you'd been giving the girl you'd scored for an entire month the most attention. You'd have plenty of time with her later. You had plenty of other girls to play with, why deprive yourself?

Nalini gave a short nod and backed away from the open door, almost in disappointment, and Astrid helpfully exited from right behind to give both girls a chance to move around.

"Jesus!" Astrid gasped as soon as she caught sight of Nalini.

"Told you there'd be a lot." Kari leaned over to get a better look and chuckled.

Emma quickly slid out of the back seat letting Nalini crawl in, before she somewhat awkwardly rearranging herself and gently lowered herself down with a shudder.

"Are you even human?" Astrid retook her seat with a snort.

You merely chuckled.

Emma soon after joined you in the front and took a

deep breath before glancing at you nervously. It was extremely reminiscent of when Nalini took that spot the first time. Hell, she even had Nalini's panties with her.

"How about you whip me out and put those to use?" You smiled warmly at Emma, partly to calm her down and partly because you were really fucking stoked to get her on your dick.

"Um, alright...." Emma looked at the panties nervously, still clutching them tightly like she was afraid of losing them.

Emma leaned over your waist and started picking at the zipper as you tried to bring your car to life.

"You can't be fucking serious!" Astrid gasped, leaning forwards to get a better look.

Just as Emma got your rapidly hardening meat free, you could feel Kari hovering over you, trying to get a gander around your head,

"I gotta admit, you've got more in you than I imagined."

"You sure that's healthy?" Astrid added, a twinge of concern coloring her voice.

"Hey. It was just soft a minute ago."

Now that she brought it up, you felt she had a point.

"For like a minute." Kari sat back down with a snort.

"I blame all of you. How is a guy supposed to go soft with so many hot chicks in his car?"

You were suddenly reminded that between your first session with Kari and your tussle with Christina you hadn't been hard for more than a few minutes at a time. You literally only had an erection while you were reminiscing about your fun with Kari.

It was a comforting thought to be reminded that there was some times when you could will your erection away. It didn't take much thought to realize that having an erection at all times could be annoying. For now though it was serving a purpose.

"What… exactly, do you want me to do… with these?" Emma hesitantly dangled the burgundy panties near your cock and looked up at you with concern.

"Hmm… I dunno. I'll leave that up to you. Just use them while you entertain me. My place isn't very far, so don't worry too much."

"... Alright...."

After a moment of consideration, Emma gently draped the cloth over your cock, eliciting a twitch from it. Emma froze and looked up at you in concern.

"That means he likes it. You're doing fine." You placed a gentle hand on Emma's head and patted her messy hair.

Emma responded by gulping hard and tenderly curling her fingers around the panties. She seemed afraid of hurting you, her grip was barely there, tickling you through the fabric.

You heard some choking from the back and Kari commented with a laugh,

"Oh god, she's precious."

"Don't be afraid to get your face in there." You placed a gentle pressure on the back of her head, just for a moment, to punctuate your words.

Emma hesitated for only a second before leaning in and taking a deep sniff.

"Hey, Nalini, how does it feel to know Emma really likes

your panties?"

At your question Emma squeaked in shock and looked up at you like you had just slapped her.

"It's what you want her to do, so I… don't know? Fine I guess." Nalini sounded confused and more focused on squirming in her seat than addressing you.

"What kind of question was that?" Astrid sounded just as confused.

"Emma here likes pussy more than dick."

Emma started sitting up, forgetting her job entirely.

"Is that why she kept checking Kari out?" Astrid mumbled behind her hand.

Emma looked panicked and near tears, her mouth working soundlessly.

"Well shit!" Kari leaned forward, "Why didn't you say something? I'd of let you cop a feel!"

And just like that her face went blank,

"Wha--?"

"Don't get the wrong idea, I'm just saying this is your first job, right? Wouldn't hurt to take initiative every once and awhile."

"I agree." Astrid leaned in, towards the gap between the seats, inches from Kari, "I'm sure our friend here would appreciate any show you could give him." With her palm facing upwards, she curled three fingers back and pointed at your meat.

Emma dumbly followed Astrid's finger and looked blankly at your throbbing cock, still wrapped in Nalini's panties.

"That's… ugh, a good point." Nalini winced and shifted in her seat, "Earn yourself brownie points. Besides, as more experienced women it's kind of our duty to help you out."

"More or less." Astrid nodded and sat back.

"The hell's wrong with you?" Kari looked Nalini up and down, sounding mildly concerned.

"Jason shoved one of my vibrators all the way up my butt." Nalini muttered as she shifted awkwardly, her ears going pink.

"Shit! Is that what that noise is?" Kari sounded significantly less concerned as she chuckled, "Anyways, Emma, right? How about his buffet is your buffet tonight? Our treat."

It took Emma a moment to answer, and when she did her voice was barely a croak,

"Yeah -- wait, I mean… maybe?" She glanced up at you.

"Well, I don't know. You haven't really done anything to earn special treatment so far…." You flicked your gaze down to your meat before looking back to the road.

It didn't take anymore to get Emma back down and pressing her soft lips against your cock, kissing slowly up and down your length.

"Oh come on, you know you'd love it!" Kari scoffed, "And none of us would mind. Right?"

"Hey! Wha--?"

Immediately the car was filled with an ear piercing shriek. It was a miracle that you manage to keep your driving straight. After everyone was done jumping in horror, Kari was left laughing like a maniac.

"Change it back!" Nalini groaned, leaning heavily on Astrid who looked sympathetic

The vibrator buried in her ass was now roaring ferociously.

Kari didn't seem to hear though, too caught up in her laughter.

"Please!" Nalini loudly squealed.

Kari ignored her as she gripped her sides and laughed.

Nalini let out a long, loud groaned before she finally screeched,

"Turn it fucking off!"

"Oh ho! I like this side of you!" Kari was momentarily shocked and significantly less giggly, but still seemed in good spirits as she reached in and fiddled with Nalini's ass.

A moment later the buzzing stopped and Nalini let out a sigh of relief.

"Thank you, uh, Kari? Sorry for the language."

"We're all big kids here." Kari scoffed and started sitting

back up straight.

"Keep that thing on medium please."

Immediately you could hear Nalini groan in defeat.

"Orders are orders." Kari let out a few more stray chuckles and wiped her eyes before leaning back down.

Emma had stopped kissing you up and down your length at this point, and perhaps taking your advice to experiment to heart, leaned down into your crotch and flicked her tongue across the only place the panties weren't covering and dragged her tongue across your balls. You twitched excitedly at that. Emma took that as her cue to start tenderly stroking you through the panty draped over you.

"So come on, let the poor girl have some fun." Kari was back to grilling you.

"I don't know about that, but I think that gives me an idea." You flicked your eyes down at Emma, who was sloppily drooling and licking your nuts, clearly inexperienced but trying, "Emma here mentioned wanting to be treated like a toy before, right?"

Nalini took a moment before grunting in agreement,

"I don't want anyone cumming without me, but maybe I'll make an exception if you use Emma."

Emma stopped her messy slurping and looked up at you in awe, spit soaking her face.

"So maybe instead of giving her a buffet, treat her like a buffet. That sounds better right."

After a moment of silence Emma squeaked out,

"Sure...." Then she leaned back down, pulled the panties off for cock and instead wrapped it around your meat and started sucking at your tip and bobbing up and down just a tiny bit.

Her lack of experience showed further, it was less a blowjob and more holstering your cock, but her eagerness more than made up for it, especially since you were just about home and didn't need her much longer.

"Haha! Someone's going to be drowning in pussy soon!" Astrid chuckled.

Kari started cackling again, and Nalini merely shifted in

her seat, looking still more concerned with the vibrator in her than anything else.

Emma didn't respond, she just pushed her face down to her fist and started flexing her hand around your cock. It was hard to tell with the noise in the back, but you could swear you could hear her laugh a tiny bit. Base on the lack of suction you were pretty sure she was smiling pretty widely at least.

There was zero suction, and whatever she was doing with her hand, while not bad, was not pleasurable, but there was a certain charm to having her so giddy with your dick in her mouth.

It was just then you pulled to a stop. Home.

"I think she likes the sound of that." You chuckled and moved your hand from her head, leaned over, and gave her small ass a hard clap and squeeze.

This time you were positive you heard a giggle.

That was the idea at least. Problem was, even if it was getting late and was already dark, there were still quite a few people milling about, even around the parking lot. Most of which looked sober, and some of which you recognized. And you'd be parading Nalini around naked.

"Hey, this is the place, isn't it?" Kari poked you in the side of the head with a scowl on her face.

"Yeah, my dorm's just a couple minute walk from here. Third floor." You muttered and shooed her hand away from your head.

Now that you really thought about it, maybe you wanted to rescind some of the orders you had given Nalini, and Kari. This wouldn't be like the bar with Kari and Astrid. That place might've been busier, but it was also full of drunk people and was a hour out of town so it would've been easy enough to avoid if thing's had turned sour. Now though…. Yes, you were pretty sure it would be okay, but what if it wasn't? Magic said it would be okay, but common sense said it wouldn't, but then, magic turned out to be real and in your back pocket at the moment.

"Then what's taking so long?" Kari sneered.

"Well maybe he's getting nervous about having us see his dorm?" Nalini cleared her throat and sat up straighter.

"Don't tell me you're getting cold feet now. You brought all of us this far, and now you're too scared to even fuck us?" Astrid managed to sound annoyed, amused and disappointed all at once.

With one last deep breath you decide. If you were doing this, it would be best to dive in head first.

"No, no, I'm just thinking up how I want to get everything up to my room." You groped around for some excuse to buy yourself a little extra time to compose yourself.

"Oh so we're thing's now?" Kari shoved her face into the front seat and curled her lip back at you.

"I bought groceries before I picked you up and now I've got Nalini's luggage to deal with." Common decency spurred you to go on the defensive, but Kari's chuckling told you how unnecessary that was.

You exhaled sharply, one part in exasperation, two parts in embarrassment. Something told you that if you planned on seeing Kari more often you were going to have to get used to her teasing you.

As you considered that speed bump, your eyes fell to Emma, currently holstering your cock with her mouth as she feebly attempted to fight off her grin and actually do something beyond keep your dick warm.

"You think you could help me with the groceries while I've got you?" You tapped her on the back of the head so she knew you were talking to her.

Emma let you out of her mouth, and with a dopey grin still on her face nodded,

"Yeah, sure. Pretty sure that's part of my job too." With a nervous chuckle she wiped some of the spit covering her cheek with her sleeve.

'Too.' You couldn't help but smile back.

With that locked down you turned in your seat and looked into the rear.

"No." Kari fixed you with a hard glare.

"What?" Your smile disappeared and you were left stunned.

"Isn't it usually just old people that get help loading their cars?" Astrid gave you a disappointed shake of her head.

Was that what she was refusing?

You weren't going to answer that, you still had one more problem to deal with.

"Hey, could you two grab Nalini for me?"

"Done." Kari's reply was just as quick as before, and she immediately reached up and honked one of Nalini's tits.

Astrid had the same idea at the exact same moments and grabbed the other with an impish smile. Nalini wasn't in the loop though and jumped in her seat.

You couldn't deny the pleasure the sight brought you, but that wasn't what you meant,

"I mean, like, work together and carry her to my room."

"What, no. Why?" Kari wrinkled her nose and sneered at you and your absurd request.

"Because I told her to crawl everywhere, and she's

professional enough to stick with it, but that's going to take longer than I feel like taking."

"Well then tell her to stop crawling."

"Where's the fun in that?"

Kari sighed and frowned at you. Astrid looked amused however.

"Please?"

Astrid and Kari both exchanged a glance, then Astrid shrugged and Kari gave another sigh, rolled her eyes, and tossed her hands up

"Yeah, fine, whatever."

"Well, okay, I guess...." Nalini nervously muttered, staring at her knees, with her hands squeezed together between her thighs.

All four doors of your car flew open in near unison. You popped the trunk as Emma made it to the back, then went back inside your car to gather up Nalini's clothes. While getting the pieces from the backseat out, you saw Nalini, having been stuck in the middle, was the last one to get out. As soon as she swung her feet out the door however, Kari grabbed onto her ankles and yanked. Nalini let out a sharp curse in surprise, nearly falling from the car, but Astrid caught her just under her breasts at the last possible moment and tucked her under her armpit. Kari did the same with Nalini's feet and then together they casually carried her over to the sidewalk to wait for you.

With Emma's help you got all the groceries in one trip and made for your dorm. Astrid and Kari were quick to follow, treating Nalini like a piece of luggage. As you passed them you took note of Nalini having her eyes squeezed tightly shut and her ears going pink.

You tried to set a measured pace, but it was hard not to run back to your dorm like a child with a new toy you were eager to play with, or rather, four new toys.

You were so excited, you didn't even notice the approaching pair of 'bros' until they were already upon you and your posse.

They had poorly disguised beers in hand and oversized sunglasses on despite it being dark outside and currently being in the dimly lit dorm lobby. They were both wearing a polo shirts, one green the other blue. Immediately they zeroed in on Emma,

"Hey there cute stuff." Green shirt nodded at her slowly.

"What are you doing out here?" Blue shirt had the biggest grin you'd ever seen.

If he was trying to be creepy, you were pretty sure he was succeeding. *You* certainly were being put off by them. They might've been drunk, or high, -- who are you kidding, in your college you'd bet money they were both -- but the real problem you had was their sunglasses made it difficult to get a full read on their facial expressions.

In what you could only assume was an act of pure instinct Emma shuffled behind you. You really weren't that imposing, but it was kind of cute that she wanted to use you as a meat shield. Well… she was cute at least, even while scared. Or maybe especially while she was scared.

"Umm, just helping bring groceries in." Emma squeaked out from behind your shoulder.

"Oh yeah?" Blue shirt sounded unnaturally interested in her simple response.

"How about you bring them back to our place? Then we can have ourselves a little party, heh heh heh…."

Green shirt started leaning incredibly close, but having to rebalance after leaning a little too far.

"Sorry, not interested." With a firm grunt you sidestepped to fully obscure Emma from his view.

Much as you'd want to claim you were being chivalrous, and that you weren't the least bit threatened by two most likely inebriated men, the fact was those were your fucking groceries and they'd have to either be pried from your cold dead hands or harvested from your stomach.

Both men looked at you, in what you believed was confusion, based on their slacken jaws, but all you could really see was your reflection in their sunglasses and you were starting to sweat. Then their attention drawn by a snicker from behind you. Immediately they both forgot about Emma and marched past you, their eye's glued to Kari's tits.

"So what's a pretty thing like you doing here all alone." Green shirts bobbed his head like a pigeon until he was in front of her.

"Yeah, sorry bud, not alone." Kari smirked and nodded towards Nalini and Astrid, both of which they had just walked past.

Seemingly for the first time, the two men noticed Astrid, and they immediately seemed to enjoy what they were seeing, their stupid grins getting bigger as they practically clawed at each other to get in front of her.

"Can't believe I missed you fine ladies." Green shirt started bobbing his head again.

"Yeah, me too…" Blue shirt added in awe.

You were pretty sure everyone had the exact same sentiment, but weren't nearly as humored as he was.

"Look, I don't want to be rude, but do you need something? We kind of have a job to do." Astrid had an apologetic smile, but her tone of voice was definitely showing signs of exhaustion.

"Oh c'mon baby, this losers groceries can wait." Blue shirt sidled up close to Astrid and wiggled his eyebrows… seductively?

Wow, fuck these guys. What did you ever do to them? You sure as fuck didn't recognize them.

"Mmhmm. Sure, she's the one doing the groceries

though," Astrid dryly muttered and pointed at Emma who waved a plastic bag filled hand meekly, "we're here to do him." She followed up by gesturing with her head down at Nalini and over to Kari, then flicking her head back towards you, bouncing her golden locks up into the air.

The two men instantly looked like they had been slapped, and their body language seemed to scream they wanted to slap you, but to your relief they decided not to even talk to you, instead Blue shirt started up with Astrid again,

"Don't worry about this jackoff. He's a big boy, he can take care of himself. Isn't that right?" He then flicked his sunglasses down his nose and looked over them at you.

Maybe he was trying to look cool, but in the end it just made him look like a little kid. His whiny tone certainly was childish.

"We're pretty big too though, probably need all four of you to help, heh heh." Green shirt smiled broadly, and even though he had sunglasses on, made zero attempt to hide his gaze straight at Kari's chest.

Emma squeaked from behind you, a look of horror on her face, but Astrid and Kari just snorted and shook their heads. Nalini however, had her head buried into Astrid side and didn't seem to be listening.

Frankly, while you were pretty upset at being verbally assaulted by a pair of complete strangers in their desperate quest for poon, hell, you were even starting to get a bit offended to the behalf of women and men alike everywhere for their caveman like tactics, but it was hard to muster up a response. You were stunned that a couple of adults could act like this, even more so that they acted like this without noticing Nalini this entire time. Eventually you managed to collect yourself enough for some kind of reply,

"Yeah, sorry, my hands are a bit full, not interested." You cut off Astrid who looked ready to say something else.

"Wasn't talking to you." One of them barked.

"Look! No one wants to fuck you perverts! Grow up and learn to read the fucking room!" Nalini pulled her face from Astrid side and screamed at the two men.

Even with their sunglasses covering nearly half their

faces it was obvious they were stunned, they were leaning away from Nalini like they were afraid she would bite.

"Wow, no need to be such a bitch." One of them weakly muttered.

"There is when I have a job to do and you're getting in the way of it! But I'm sure neither of you would know *anything* about that! A couple of wannabe frat bro's like you haven't worked a day in their damn lives! You just mooch off your middle class parents without a care in the world!"

"H-hey! We've got jobs!" Green shirt tried to straighten up and puff out his chest.

A moment later he was deflated by a glare from Nalini,

"Oh yeah, let me guess, flipping burgers? Maybe mopping floors? I'm *real* impressed. I'm sure you're just in this cheap school for fun because you've got you future made for you right? Heh, shirt, I bet you *are* here just for fun aren't you?" Nalini paused, but the men already looked broken, probably why she paused, to make it hurt more, "If you're creepy lines and whining like baby's didn't impress us I'd say we're all soaking wet now!"

You felt that some of Nalini's bite should've been dulled by her nudity, her dried and cracking cum facial, and her current, horizontal, orientation, but both men looked cowed.

"Are we done?" You could practically hear the smirk in Astrid's voice.

"No one want's you and we're all kind of busy right now." Kari readjusted Nalini's feet under her arm and tilted her head at the two men.

Both of them looked towards you and Emma for a moment, still at a loss for words. Emma beside you was frantically shaking her head.

"Uh, yeah… so, ladies? We've got a few stairs to climb." You jabbed a thumb over your shoulder once you caught everyone's attention.

You couldn't deny that some of what Nalini said hurt you too, particularly about the school you currently attended, but at the same time you couldn't really deny all of it either. But most of all you were stunned at her downright feral transformation.

In your mind you considered telling the men off yourself, to strike the finishing blow of sorts, but your gut told you keeping this conversation going after it turned sour wouldn't help anyone, and your dick was screaming at you that you could be fucking right now. All were compelling arguments, but you weren't a filthy communist, so majority rules.

"Lead the way." Astrid turned her head with a sniff.

You did just that. As you approached the stairwell, from the corner of your eye you saw Emma twist her head around frequently. Your stomach twisted. There was a reason you didn't want to take the elevator, it displayed the floor you stopped at, but as you followed Emma's gaze behind you, your fears were assuages. Both men were already starting to head back towards the front door, their original destination, but not before one parting shot,

"I hope your dick falls off, asshole!"

"The fuck did I do." You shook your head as you took the first step up.

Astrid, Kari and Emma all began to laugh.

"Well I guess you don't technically need to be smart to

be in college." Astrid clicked her tongue behind you.

"Yeah, but seems like a basic life skill to learn when you can and can't hit on someone, like when they're working!" Emma sighed, and dropped her shoulders, then glanced up at you with a smile.

"Or at least learn to take a hint instead of forcing us to go nuclear, eh?" Kari was still chuckling when you heard the first clap.

Glancing over your shoulder you saw she was giving Nalini couple firm pats just above her knee,

"But I'm impressed with you Mr, Stamina, you kept your cool back there better than I would've guessed."

"Is that seriously the nickname you're going with?" You put on a pained smile only Emma could see and shook your head.

"It's a work in progress."

"Yeah, well, seemed to me you ladies had things under control." Years of living with your sisters taught you that admitting you weren't being cool, just confused as hell, would only leave you open for ridicule.

"Still though, didn't think this one had that in her!" Kari chuckled and Astrid joined in soon after.

"Mr, Thornton I don't want to be rude, but if you don't hurry I don't think I'll be able to hold on for you." Nalini began let out a low groan and you could see her squeezing and flexing her ass.

That explained her short fuse you suppose…

Spurred by the reminder of what you had on the line, you picked up the pace. In no time at all, you made it to your front door and after unlocking it, kicked it open.

"Bedroom's that way." You let Kari and Astrid cart Nalini in first.

"Ugh, what's that smell?" Kari grimaced as soon as the door was open.

"Smells like your bar…." Astrid sounded equally unappreciative.

"It smells like beer and piss!" Kari barked back as they made it to the end of the hall and turned towards your room.

"Fine, it smells like the *bathroom* of your bar."

Kari responded by clicking her tongue and gesturing with her head towards where you had pointed them.

As was your ritual, you dropped your pants at the door and shook off your shoes, but it wasn't with nearly as much pleasure as you had hoped.

"Um, where should I put these?" Emma lifted the plastic shopping bags up, her gaze drifting down to your crotch.

"Just leave them somewhere in the kitchen and meet me in my room."

It was kind of humiliating to think you'd been living in piss stink for so long you had just gotten used to it, but it was also nothing plenty of sex couldn't remedy. You'd just deal with the smell some other time.

You left Nalini's bags in the meagre living space in the center of the room and went about gathering the supplies you'd need for your fun, among them being Nalini's sex toys. It was pretty obvious which one was the 'big one' as soon as you extracted both dildos. Even the 'small one' honestly put you to shame, but you were somewhat awed by the size of the larger one.

Well, you weren't about to be jealous of some plastic,

but it certainly meant you had a lot to live up to.

With your supplies collected you marched into your bedroom. You dumped the toys and your underpants near the doorway and crept towards the bed with the remainder of your tools in hand.

"...I *know* they were *so* desperate!"

"Well wouldn't you be too if you were them? How much tail do you think they get with their attitude."

Astrid and Kari was already reclining on your bed, facing each other and chatting away.

"Keep going! Yes! Mmm! Don't stop!" Beside Kari, Nalini was on her back, legs up in the air and was grinding her crotch against Emma's face while grabbing a couple fistfuls of hair.

"Enjoying yourself without me are we?" You walked up and gave Emma a smack across her ass, causing her to yelp in surprise.

"He's here now, hurry up!" Nalini sounded desperate and pulled Emma's face deeper into her crotch, and started grinding with much more vigor.

"Was anyone that desperate when *we* were in college?" Astrid muttered, paying you no mind as you crept up behind Kari.

"Are you kidding? Remember that one scrawny band geek? What's his face?"

Astrid threw back her head and groaned at the reminder, giving a wry chuckle all the while, just as you grabbed hold of one of Kari's ankles and pulled her to the edge of the bed.

"Hey!" Kari yelped and wound up for a kick.

You quickly wrapped your arm around her legs in response, squeezing them together, just as recognition dawned on her face and Kari relaxed with a tired obscenity. You wasted no time taking the belt you had recovered from your pants and looping it around her ankles. It was a double ring belt, luckily, so you didn't have holes and a pin to deal with and you could make it nice and tight. There was a decent tail left that wasn't exactly pretty, but it did it's job effectively.

"What are you doing?" Kari looked up at you in confusion and wiggled her blue loafers slowly, testing her bindings.

"Tying you up." You released her now wrapped ankles and reached up to flip her over.

"Oof, yeah, I figured. Not what I meant. Hey!" Kari didn't resist as you flipped her over, but didn't seem particularly happy when you grabbed her arms.

She put in a pittance of a fight, but you quickly straddled her back then twisted both her hands behind her back and pinned her wrists together. You wasted to time getting to work tying her wrists together with the laces from one of your shoes.

"Seemed like a hot idea." You grunted simply.

"Ah, I get it." Kari couldn't turn her head around enough to see you, but she relaxed considerably at the explanation.

Just then Nalini let out a long moan and squeezed her thighs together around Emma's head, her own head flung back in ecstasy.

"Plus after I saw how those guy's rubbed you the wrong way I figured it's be a good idea to do something you might like."

Kari scoffed,

"This and that are different."

"I'm fucking you, they wanted to." Your voice was colored with your confusion.

Before you got a response, you repositioned yourself so you could get to Kari's legs and wrap your other length of shoelaces around her knees.

"Well yeah, but this is work, they were hitting on us."

"But it's still sex one way or another, correct?" With one final tug you finished with your last knot.

You were no sailor, and you were using makeshift supplies that just barely did their job, but you were pretty sure Kari wouldn't be getting free unless she really wrenched on her bindings for a little while.

Kari sighed and buried her face into your bed sheets.

"Why would any of us want to sleep with desperate losers for fun?" Astrid butt in, her tone suggesting you thought you were a child or an idiot.

"Ouch." You winced, getting off Kari, "I didn't realize you thought this way about me."

"How have you gotten this far in life without getting it?" Kari growled and huffed, twisting around and rolling onto her back.

"You're fine." Nalini was panting, and finally released Emma from the grip of her thighs, "You've kept things professional so far and I'm sure I speak for us all when I say it's appreciated," Nalini paused to catch her breath some more, but no one interrupted, " it's just work is work and pleasure is pleasure, there can be some overlap, but at the end of the day they're not the same."

"Awe, so you're saying you don't like what I'm putting you through?" You tossed off your shirt, your last piece of clothing as you pretended to sound hurt.

"No one said that." Nalini sat up quickly with a yelp.

"Hey, we'll see how you do, but I like me a resourceful guy." Kari purred, testing her bindings for affect.

Astrid rolled her eyes and Emma looked down at her knees with a flush to her cheeks. Nalini looked relieved and nodded in agreement.

"Maybe I can convince you to come back to my place *after* work sometime then." You grinned and rubbed your hands together.

"Let's not get ahead of ourselves here." Kari quickly went on the defensive, sitting up and staring you down with a steely look in her eye.

You quickly put up you hands and conceded you weren't trying to be 'unprofessional' and Kari quickly gave you a satisfied nod.

It was incredibly clear that whatever you wallet did to their perception, 'normal sex' was just that and 'paid sex' was very different. But you were going to do your damndest to make sure tonight you'd have conclusive evidence that you could tear down that wall with clever efforts.

You'd asked them some questions about their likes and dislikes to mixed, and rather lackluster results, but now you could try whatever you wanted out and see how the girls would react. It certainly would be fun to play with all of them, but Astrid and Emma specifically were the most mysterious. Emma told you a little bit about what she thought she'd like, but she was either too embarrassed to say much, or just didn't know enough about herself to give you a proper checklist to go through. And Astrid... you got the impression she didn't like you a whole lot, she mostly just tolerated you.

Following that train of thought, you got off of Kari and pounced at Astrid who up until then had been watching you, looking somewhat bored. Astrid immediately recoiled and let out some unintelligible grunt, perhaps even a Swedish curse for all you knew, as you bowled her onto her back.

With one hand on either side of her head, sinking deep into your bed, you leaned in for a kiss.

Astrid still seemed stunned by you crashing into her that it took her a moment to realize what you were after and when she did she tried to retreat into the mattress. It was fruitless, obviously, a moment later your lips were on hers.

Her crimson lips were closed tight, but that didn't stop you. You ran your tongue across the warm, tender wall and we're rewarded quickly by them parting to let your tongue inside. Without a moment's hesitation you snaked your tongue into her mouth and started feeling around. You ran your tongue over her lips and teeth and swabbed the inside of her cheek, you poked and prodded at her tongue and took in her flavor.

It wasn't at all satisfying though. You could taste her, and it was arousing you to no end, but you weren't satisfied. If you had to guess at why, you'd say it was probably the poorly masked look of disgust on her face, and her general lack of any reciprocation. If you wanted that you'd have just went straight between her legs.

At least you were learning something already. Astrid didn't like being kissed. It compounded with what you already knew, just because you could do something, didn't mean it had to be liked or even tolerated. All that meant to you though was that by the end of the night you wanted Astrid to be more than happy to kiss you back, maybe even let you hit on her after everything was said and done. Shit, if you could fuck her into dating you that would be the greatest success you could imagine! All things considered though you weren't sure how comfortable you'd be going steady with anyone….

Before any of that even mattered though it would've been smart to stop making out with her.

Since Astrid didn't like having your tongue in her mouth you pulled back and instead buried your face into her neck and pressed your entire naked form into her. Her reaction was nearly as bad as when you jumped her. As soon as you placed your lips on her neck she flinched, her head and shoulder squeezed together in a weak attempt at defending against you and she put a hand on your chest. She seemed to think better of pushing you off of her, but it was obvious she was considering it.

"So… um, Emma? You go to school around here too?" Astrid shakily asked, her nose wrinkled and her jaw tensed.

You moved up a little, pulling your lips off her neck with a wet smack, and pinched her earlobe between your lips.

"Well not here." Emma coughed.

The feeling of the bed sinking slightly and shaking told you Emma had left the space between Nalini's thighs and taken up a spot close to you, as did the volume of her continuation,

"I go to the high school across town. I'm in my last year."

"R-right… I think you may have mentioned that…." Astrid's voice was strained.

So she definitely didn't like you slobbering on any part of her head, at least not yet, so you'd have to go lower. Not that you planned on going for her scalp next. You sat up, still straddling Astrid's waist, and started looking for a way to undo her corset.

"So how's that treating you?" Kari added to the conversation, smirking at you with a cocked eyebrow before rolling over and devoting her attention Emma.

You couldn't find a way to undo her corset. The front of the garment had laces weaving back and forth like a spider web up the entire length, but you couldn't find any end to the string. Logically that probably meant you should check the back, but the more you thought, the more you considered that you'd just be doing more of the same. If she didn't like your mouth near her face or neck would her breasts be all that different? Possibly. But maybe a complete change of tactics would be smarter. You had planned on getting her to like you after all.

"Uh… it's not bad I suppose." Emma bobbed her head from side to side, her attention was split between Kari and what you were doing.

Perhaps it would've been a bit on the nose, but you slid of Astrid and moved to expose her nether's. It was a tight fit, but you managed to squeeze your fingers underneath the waistband of her pants and slowly started to peel them down.

"You, uh, don't have any troubles with any of your subjects?" Kari twitched in her makeshift bindings.

"Oh like you give a shit about that." Astrid scoffed and lifted herself off the bed just enough to let you pull her pants down.

You could actually feel it separating from her skin, if the room was quiet you were sure you could hear it, it was like her pants were vacuum packed.

"What Kari really wants to know is how much shit you

get for being a lesbian." Astrid lowered herself back to the bed once you had her pants down to her knees. She had definitely relaxed some now that you didn't have your lips on her.

She had practically been vacuum packed into her pants. No doubt that was the reason she had a gold g-string thong on instead of actually panties, there wasn't enough room for anything more. The particular style of g-string even managed to put the one you had found in Nalini's hotel to shame.

"It's called tact you bitch, learn it!" Kari looked over her shoulder and scowled at Astrid.

"It's fine, I don't care!" Emma sat up straight, her eyes nearly popping from her head.

"She's right though, I want the juicy deets." Kari no longer sounded the least bit upset.

"Uh…oh… um." Emma sucked on her lips for a moment, then looked up at you and blinked a few times.

All you could do was smile and shrug at her. You were getting used to Kari's boisterous personality, and Emma would have to as well. It stood to reason Astrid had a very similar disposition as her friend.

"I mean, sure. Or well… I… don't get bullied… so…."

"Seriously? High school must've changed since I was your age." Astrid's eyebrows crept up her head.

"Well… no one really knows I like girls." Emma's eyes dropped back down to where you were working on Astrid's crotch, but her eyes were narrowed and her nose was wrinkled. She seemed lost in thought.

You slipped your hand beneath the top of the panties and pinched Astrid's lower lips between the sides of your first and middle finger. Her reaction this time was far less violent. Her back arched ever so slightly, her nostrils flared and her chest rose as she sucked in a deep breath, but beyond that there was nothing. You seriously doubted it was entirely because she was now paying attention to Emma. This was a good sign.

"I'm not buying it." Kari clicked her tongue.

"Complete bullshit." Astrid made a show of clearing her throat.

"I have to agree. If a girl as cute as you didn't date any guys for three years, in high school no less, people would suspect something." Nalini let out a wistful sigh, sprawled out and spent beside Emma, "No way hormonal teenagers you stay away from you."

Astrid and Kari voiced their agreement. When Emma looked around and met your gaze you gave her a wink and a bob of your eyebrows.

"Oh… um… I have guy friends." Emma's gaze dropped to the rooms carpet, her face turning beet red.

Now that you knew Astrid was a bit more comfortable without your spit being involved, you had a thread of follow. Keeping up the pressure, you slowly pulled your hand back and tracing the outer edge of her slit. No matter how much you rubbed her though, her reaction was nonexistent unless you counted the increase in moisture. You'd have to do something about that.

"I… uh, also had a couple boyfriends." Emma murmured, just above a whisper, rubbing her hands up and down her thighs.

"No shit?" Kari lifted her head of the bed in a show of interest, before letting it bounce back down.

Nalini too looked interested as she sat part way up, supporting herself by throwing her arms behind her.

Astrid seemed to be trying to do the same as Nalini, but you reached back and pressed into her chest with one hand. With the hand still buried in her panties you felt around for her clit, once you found it, you braced one finger beside it and with the other started to trace over it. Just as you hoped, Astrid was having much more trouble keeping her composure. Her body went limp and her eyes shot open wide. It still wasn't quite what you were after though.

"Yeah, I dated a couple of my friends -- I mean now they're friends." Emma took a deep breath.

"This before you figured out you like girls? Or were you just putting on a show?" Kari's question was met with a grunt of agreement from Nalini.

You were still focused on trying to get Astrid to squirm though. You increased the pressure you were using and slowly extended your finger, running the length of it over her clit. That caused her to squeeze her eyes shut for a moment and suck on her lips.

"Um, sort of." Emma took another deep breath and flopped backwards onto your bed, "I liked these guys that's why we're' still friends, and well… I thought dating them would work but… it just didn't feel right.

Y'know?"

You took a few more moments to trace your fingers around the edge of Astrid's slit, but she seemed to be getting used to whatever you did to her, as she was starting to rein in her reactions considerably, she was even back up to asking questions,

"Didn't feel right how? Like with sex or…?"

"No, not exactly." Emma shook her head frantically, "Like, we kissed and stuff, but it just didn't feel right. I'm not sure how to describe it."

"Maybe they just sucked at kissing." Kari sniffed loudly.

It seemed like making Astrid squirm with just your hands was going to be an uphill battle from here on, so you decided to go back to finding out what else she liked. As soon as you pulled your hands from her panties you could swear she let out a sigh, but her expression hadn't changed from the friendly smile she was giving Emma. You decided to keep on with your plans, rolling down her panties to her knees for later and went to flip her over,

"That's an idea. How'd they kiss you?" Astrid nodded her head at Emma, and gave you a momentary look you couldn't quite decipher, her brow was furrowed slightly, but she was still smiling as she helped you flip her onto her stomach.

Sure as shit, the laces to her corset were on the back.

"I don't know." Emma laughed nervously, "I guess they were really gentle, loving maybe…." Emma laughed and brought a hand to her chin, "I told one of them I liked the idea of having my neck sucked on though, and he tried that a few times…" Emma cleared her throat but no one was stopping her so she pressed on, "but I had the girl I dated do it and I nearly came right there." Emma started laughing again and squeezed her eyes shut while shaking her head.

Once you peeled the corset off Astrid, as well as a matching black tube top that she had been wearing underneath it, you took a moment to admire her back. She must've worked out, that much you were vaguely aware of.

You were reminded of something. Your college had a lot of rotating workshops available and one year you got a masseuse certification. It had been a lust filled attempt at getting to rub down attractive women. The truth ended up being that most of the other students that you had to practice with were either old, hairy, or men though. Still, there had been a few attractive students that you had the luck of being paired with a few times but you couldn't remember a damn thing about their back.

If someone asked you what you thought about a woman's back you probably wouldn't have been able to answer. Here and now though you found something irresistible about Astrid's toned and defined back. The definition of her shoulder blades and the gentle valley in the middle of her spine that spoke of the size of some abdominal muscles you didn't know the name of. Having her before you, completely free to do what you willed with, you didn't hesitate to trace every curve and line on her back. To your pleasant surprise you felt her shiver, more than once. You got the biggest reaction when you ran your fingers down the length of the crease in the middle of her back, but you also got a bit of a reaction when you traced the large dimples she had right above each of her tight and defined cheeks.

"Oh, w-well maybe they did suck then." Astrid cleared her throat and clenched her cheeks together, really showing you how toned they were as well, "how many people have you dated?"

"Uhhh, two guys and one girl." Emma sat up, her flush finally starting to die down as she was beginning to get into the rhythm of things.

"Sound's like my last threesome." Kari fought and struggled for a moment until she managed to sit up, despite the stunted use of her arms and legs.

"So maybe you just haven't met the right guy then." Astrid sucked in a deep breath ending with a grunt as you dug your thumbs in between her clenched cheeks and started to pry.

'Pry' was the perfect word for it as well. It was pretty clear she worked out, just by appearances, Nalini had a nice ass and Kari was just naturally thick, but Astrid's rear looked like it had been sculpted from marble, and now that you were trying to spread her cheeks they felt like marble too.

"I'm not trying to sounds homophobic or anything!" Astrid quickly added, relaxing enough for you to finally get her cheeks apart, "I just mean if you've got doubts maybe -- eep -- there's a reason." Astrid looked over her shoulder to glare at you after you had brushed your thumb over her backdoor and gotten her to squeal.

"I've gotta agree with Miss Piggy. You said your boyfriends were 'gentle' but in my opinion, if you're trying to compare the two, there's one thing you want men for over women in the bed, it's a good brutal pounding."

Astrid had immediately reached out to give Kari a jab to the shoulder, just as you had thrusted your thumb into her ass. You immediately felt her entire body tense underneath you.

"Fucking shit! What the hell?" Kari yelped and rolled away from Astrid, a grimace on her face.

Emma immediately scoot away, into Nalini who was sitting up straight now, both looked stunned.

"Will you just pick a goddamn hole already!" Astrid buried her face into the bed and groaned.

With a pained smile, Kari let out a brief chuckle and glanced down at the thumb you had sunk into Astrid's ass.

"Eventually." You made no move to stop however, you actually started working your thumb in deeper.

"Astrid here doesn't like being teased." Kari shook her

head slowly.

As Kari's tone and demeanor softened, Emma and Nalini both exhaled slowly and slumped over. Nalini still kept a wary eye on Astrid, but Emma had her eyes locked on Nalini's naked form and was shuffling away frantically.

"How's she feel about having things up her butt?" You flexed your thumb one last time and then slowly pulled it out.

"Kari!" Astrid snapped her head to the side and glared at her friend.

Kari made no attempt to hide her vicious smile though,

"How about you try something bigger and find out?"

Astrid immediately let out a hiss and pushed off the bed, nearly knocking you over as she got on her knees and towered over Kari.

"Fuck off, you slugged me out of nowhere, now you've got to pay for it."

Astrid immediately deflated and her eyes fell to your rock hard cock. It was difficult to read her expression, her body language screamed crestfallen, but her in her eyes popped with liveliness. On the one hand none of her reactions was anything like when you tried to kiss her, but on the other hand she looked ready to slug Kari on purpose for recommending you take her ass.

Scary as it was to even consider trying anything she might not like after nearly breaking your thumbs trying to pry her buns apart, it was incredibly tempting.

"Maybe in a little bit." You gave Astrid a broad smile.

Her face was still blank. No disappointment, no relief, no scowl, no anything. That didn't help.

"Since you had your chance to tell me what you liked and disliked earlier." Your smiled faltered.

This time Astrid gave a wry smile, and swayed her head from side to side.

Heading back to the doorway from among Nalini's sex toys, you pulled out one of the other supplies you had gathered together, the moisturizer you had bought from Christina earlier in the afternoon.

"For now though, you think you could hold her down and lube her up for me?" You jiggled the pink bottle towards Astrid and flicked your eyes towards Kari.

"The fuck did I do?"

Astrid seemed unimpressed by both you and her friend's protests, still not helping you figure out how she was feeling.

"Y'know, before I take you for a spin?" You tried to do something to get a read on her.

Her response was to smile, but also to snatch the bottle from your hands and pounce on Kari. Immediately, the two started to wrestle. Kari was losing, badly, in large part due to her being bound. It was to your surprise that the shoelaces were holding up tremendously well. You were a bit disappointed though that you couldn't tell if Astrid was smiling because you had told her you wanted her ass, or because she wanted to give Kari a hard time.

Within moments Astrid had Kari on her stomach and dropped a knee onto her head, shoving it deep into your mattress. For a moment you froze with concern at how violent it looked, but a moment later a muffled grumble washed away your fears,

"You better hope he fucks me stupid or the second I get

these things off--" Kari was immediately cut off by a hard downward slap against one of her cheeks from Astrid, and she gave a muffled squeal.

"Who's Miss Piggy now? You look and sound like a pig!" Astrid let out a short laugh, but quickly sobered up as Kari started to buck and squirm underneath her while cursing up a storm.

Astrid was forced to move her knee from the back of Kari's head and instead use both her knees to hold Kari's head in place, while leaning over and grabbing onto her wrists.

"You don't mind helping me with this, do you?" Astrid was looking straight at Emma.

"Uh… no." Emma swallowed audibly.

"Just get her pants off and spread her cheeks for me."

Kari had calmed down as soon as Emma grabbed her pants but Astrid didn't let go.

You turned to Nalini, who up until this point was just watching things with a mildly amused look on her face, and you bought one finger to your mouth and with the other gestured for her to roll over herself.

Nalini's eyes went wide and her jaw went slack, she looked like she wanted to say something, but after a beat she shut her mouth and did as you asked. As you reached for Nalini you heard an audible creak and a pop as Astrid opened the plastic bottle you had given her.

"What is that? It smells pretty good." Emma coughed, one of Kari's generous cheeks in each hand.

"Says it's some tropical bullshit." Astrid barely even glanced at the label before pressed the opening against Kari's opening and started to squeeze.

"Fuck that's cold!"

You couldn't say the same about the vibrator you had begun to extract from Nalini. It was warmed to her body temperature.

Nalini collapsed against the bed and bit onto the covers in an attempt to muffle her sigh of relief once the toy was finally removed from her. You didn't know the exact feeling, but you did know that after a while you could get used to a constant sensation to the point where having it stop was a shock of its own.

"Why do you even have this?" Astrid looked up at you

and pulled the bottle away from Kari's hole.

Emma was completely focused on tenderly spreading the cream around with her thumbs.

"For lube." You coughed and twirled the vibrator around.

"Why not get actual lube?"

"This is less conspicuous."

"Do you even have a roommate?"

What the fuck were you supposed to tell her? You bought it so a stranger would fuck you and you could avoid looking like a sexual predator?

The best you could do was shake your head and try to change the subject.

"Hey, Emma, that's enough I think, I can do the rest."

It took until you placed a hand on her shoulder, causing her to jump, before she got the message.

To your pleasure you noticed that Kari couldn't really see with Astrid pinning her head.

Once Emma got out of the way, you straddled Kari's hips and readied the currently silent vibrator. You smiled broadly at what you saw. You had left a somewhat impressive bruise on one of Kari's cheeks from the night before, and by coincidence that was what Astrid had hit and caused Kari to squeal.

You began pushing the vibrator in. Surprisingly, she was taking it just as well as Nalini had.

"Jesus, how much of you is there." Kari grumbled from between Astrid's legs.

It took everything you had not to burst out laughing, Astrid went as far as biting her lip to keep quiet.

Once you had the toy deep enough, you turned it on low.

"And where the fuck did you learn that!" Kari let out a gasp, and you definitely heard a bit of a chuckle.

The jig was clearly up and Astrid burst out laughing as she released Kari.

You only needed a moment to decide to up the power some more.

"Jesus!" Kari wiggled underneath you in a superficial attempt to get away, but putting your hands on her ass and pressing down was enough to stop it entirely, "This feels weird. I don't think I've ever had a vibrator this far up my ass before."

You were somewhat surprised, your impression of Kari thus far was that she was a wild and experienced party girl, at least at one point. Then again, she said 'this far.'

"Well consider this a treat then." You started to knead her cheeks then squeezed them together around the vibrator, "After all, you told me you wanted me to break you, right?"

"Oh, is that what this is about?" Kari lifted her head from the bed and looked back at you, "Well it feels weird but you're going to need more--"

You flicked the toy up to max.

"--Turn it the fuck off!" Kari's tune changed in an instance and she buried her face back into your bed with a low groan.

"You thought it was funny when you did it to Nalini." You followed up with a mighty crack across her, so far, unbruised cheek.

Kari arched her back and moaned, then shakily added,

"I thought, ugh, she was overreacting."

You quickly got off Kari and slipped a hand under her, lifting her onto her knees by her neck, forcing her to look up at you as you towered over her, then squeezed,

"Oh, so you're broken already, bitch?" You gave her another hard slap across her pale ass.

"Fuck you." She wheezed.

You started to squeeze harder and gave her another harder smack, this one forcing Kari's jaw to work soundlessly for a moment.

"I think I should give you a matching set."

"I think… I'm starting to like you." Kari gasped out with what little air you hadn't cut off yet.

With a smirk of your own you leaned in and started to viciously tongue her mouth. She was kissing you back almost instantly. When you drew back a moment later there was a trail of spit connecting you. You didn't let her go until you spat your mixed saliva back into her mouth, then you tossed her back against the bed.

You were starting to really want to bone her, but at the same time you had other plans.

"Hey Emma, where are we on that roughing you up idea?"

Emma just stared at you, her eyes periodically flicked between your rock hard cock pointed straight at her and Kari who was recovering from a short coughing fit.

"There's a middle ground, I don't need to do all that." You quickly added.

"Umm… sure, I guess." Emma let out a half cough half chuckle and started to pull her shirt off over her head.

She barely tossed the shirt to the side before you shoved her onto her back and pinned her beneath you. Emma's reaction was to squeak and go limp. She clearly wasn't a fighter like Astrid or Kari. Her natural submissiveness made it easy to treat her 'like a toy' as she had mentioned liking the idea of earlier in the afternoon.

You pressed into her and grabbed a fistful of her soft hair, tilting her head back forcefully and slipped her your tongue. After a moment's hesitation she tried to kiss you back, but even that was limp.

You tightened your grip on her hair and pulled her in deeper, taking a moment to bite her lip and pulled it back. Despite her meek reciprocations, she responded by let out a moan between breaths and placing a hand on the back of your head.

As she ran her hands through your hair, you moved your free hand down to her chest and rolled up her bra, exposing her adorably small breasts. Taking to heart the suggestion she might like thing's rough you pinched one of her nipples tight and yanked back on it.

Emma froze and yelped. The reaction shocked you into stopping and letting her breast go. You started to pull back, but Emma quickly grabbed a fistful of your hair and growled at you,

"Do it again!" She then pulled your face towards hers and started kissing you with far more vigor than before.

You couldn't tell if she had just gotten over her nerves or if you awoke something in her, but you weren't going to complain. You pushed your hips between her legs and started to grind against her through her pants and kneaded her breasts with reckless abandon. No matter how rough you got though, Emma didn't pull her tongue out of your mouth for more than a second.

Eventually you felt Emmas thighs clamp around yours as one of her hands snaked down into her pants.

That was certainly an idea. Exploring Astrid ended up being more of an experiment and an appreciation for her body than anything, but Emma was getting you real hot and heavy. Experimentation was fun in its own way, but there would be time for that later. Then again, there'd be time for sex later too.

Decisions, decisions.

End of Book One